HOW TO RAISE AN ELEPHANT

As the temperature rises in Gaborone, Precious Ramotswe, founder of the No. 1 Ladies' Detective Agency, wonders whether the heat could be the reason that business is particularly slow. Precious has time to contemplate her new neighbours, who have a rather volatile relationship . . . But then a distant cousin of Mma Ramotswe's comes to the agency with a plea for help. Armed with Mma Ramotswe's circumspection and Mma Makutsi's sharp eye, they proceed with confidence and open hearts. What, after all, could be more straightforward than a family matter? Meanwhile, their colleague Charlie is behaving oddly, borrowing Mma Ramotswe's van and returning it in an unusual condition. Digging a little deeper, the explanation is both strange and extraordinary, and takes Charlie, along with Mma Ramotswe's husband, Mr J. L. B. Matekoni, on a hair-raising night-time expedition.

HOW TO RAISE AN ELEPHANT

ALEXANDER McCALL SMITH

LARGE
PRINT

First published in Great Britain 2020
by
Little, Brown
an imprint of Little, Brown Book Group

First Isis Edition
published 2021
by arrangement with
Little, Brown Book Group
an Hachette UK Company

A catalogue record for this book is available
from the British Library.

ISBN 978–1–78541–940–9

Published by
Ulverscroft Limited
Anstey, Leicestershire

Set by Words & Graphics Ltd.
Anstey, Leicestershire
Printed and bound in Great Britain by
T J Books Ltd., Padstow, Cornwall

This book is printed on acid-free paper

This book is for Mats and Cecilia Ögren Wanger,
Swedish friends of Botswana.

CHAPTER
ONE

No Double Bed

Precious Ramotswe, owner and only begetter of the No. 1 Ladies' Detective Agency — established to deal with the problems of ladies, and others — looked across her office towards the desk occupied by Grace Makutsi, former secretary and distinguished graduate — with ninety-seven per cent in the final examinations — of the Botswana Secretarial College. The sun was streaming through the high window behind Mma Ramotswe's desk, sending a narrow butter-yellow beam to illuminate small particles of floating dust, just perceptible, feather-light, moving up and down, sometimes sliding sideways in obedience to the invisible currents in the room. But for the most part the air was still — it being that sort of day, sluggish and non-committal. The sort of day on which something might happen, but was more likely not to.

It was not unusual for Mma Ramotswe to look up and see Mma Makutsi staring back at her; and the same thing might be said for Mma Makutsi, who would suddenly lift her gaze from the papers in front of her and notice Mma Ramotswe watching her thoughtfully. Neither minded this — indeed, both were used to it, and when either of them was out of the office for whatever reason, the other would find that she missed seeing her colleague there at her desk when she looked up. This was particularly true for Mma Makutsi, for whom Mma Ramotswe was a reassuring presence every bit as significant, every bit as reassuring, as the great rock dome of Kgale Hill on the outskirts of town, or the deep waters of the Limpopo River, just a few hours off to the east, or the sandhills of the Kalahari over to the west. These were all geographical facts, just as Mma Ramotswe herself seemed to be a geographical fact. She was simply there — as predictable and as constant as any of these things. And her voice was as familiar and as loved as the voice of the doves inhabiting the acacia tree behind Tlokweng Road Speedy Motors; indeed, she would not have been surprised had Mma Ramotswe suddenly started to coo, just as those doves did. Mma Makutsi could not imagine Botswana without those doves, and she could not imagine it without Mma Ramotswe; if she were not there, then it would be just any other country; with her it was something special — it was Mma Ramotswe's place, a place bathed in the warmth of her presence as effectively as the sun blesses the land each morning with its warming rays.

Now Mma Ramotswe looked across the office and noticed that Mma Makutsi was looking back at her. There was something different about Mma Makutsi, she thought, and it took Mma Ramotswe a little while to work out what it was. It was not what she was wearing: she had on the green dress that for some reason she liked to wear on Fridays — Mma Makutsi was a creature of habit. No, it was something else, and when Mma Ramotswe realised what it was she reproached herself for not noticing it at once. Mma Makutsi's glasses, normally large and round, like outsize swimming goggles, had shrunk. They were still round, but the lenses were considerably smaller — tiny discs, by comparison, no bigger than the coins to be found in a pocket of small change. Any detective worth her salt would have spotted the change immediately, thought Mma Ramotswe. She had always prided herself on her powers of observation, but it was hardly very observant to miss a detail such as this. Of course, she had the excuse of the familiar: the eye is lulled into complacency when contemplating those things and people we see every day.

"Your glasses, Mma," said Mma Ramotswe.

Mma Makutsi leaned back in her chair. She was smiling. "I wondered when you were going to notice, Mma. Do you like them? They're new."

Mma Ramotswe knew from long experience that Mma Makutsi was sensitive to criticism. The only response one could safely give if asked one's opinion on any aspect of her appearance was to say that it was perfect. Any reservation, even in the form of a momentary hesitation, could give rise to a display of hurt feelings that could quickly become a more than momentary sulk; not prolonged beyond the evening, of course — Mma Ramotswe had never known Mma Makutsi to keep a state of huff going for more than a

3

few hours, but it was best to avoid such occasions altogether, she thought.

"They are very fine glasses," she said. "They are clearly very fashionable."

It was just the right thing to say. Mma Makutsi touched the spectacles gently, repositioning them slightly on the bridge of her nose. "I saw them in a magazine, Mma," she said. "One of those very famous actresses was wearing them."

"Which famous actress, Mma?"

Mma Makutsi shrugged. "Oh, I don't remember the names of any of those people. But they are very famous, Mma. They go to parties and there are many photographers at those parties. Snap, snap, snap — so that we can all see what was happening at the party even if we never get an invitation."

"So, this lady — whoever she was — was wearing your spectacles, Mma?"

"The exact same," said Mma Makutsi. "And there was a list at the bottom of the page of what she was wearing, and how much it cost. They gave the name of the shop where you could order spectacles like that. It's down in Cape Town; they do not sell these glasses in Botswana. You have to write off for them. These are Cape Town glasses — everyone is wearing them down there, they say."

Mma Ramotswe wondered whether it was really a model who had been wearing them. "I think that lady might have been paid to wear them, Mma. I think that is possible, because otherwise they would not have published the details of where you could buy them."

4

"It does not matter," said Mma Makutsi. "She might have been a model — who knows?"

Mma Ramotswe thought about this. "If she was a model, Mma, do you think she was really short-sighted, or would she have been wearing them just for the photograph?"

Mma Makutsi hesitated. "It is possible, Mma, that she was short-sighted. I could not tell from the photograph."

"You're right, though, Mma," said Mma Ramotswe. "It doesn't matter whether or not she needed them. The point is: they look very good on you, Mma."

"You're not just saying that, Mma?"

Mma Ramotswe shook her head. "I am not just saying it, Mma Makutsi. I am sitting here thinking it as well. I am sitting here thinking: those spectacles look very good on Mma Makutsi. They are a big improvement."

As soon as she said this, Mma Ramotswe realised that she had said the wrong thing. She was about to rephrase her words, but it was too late.

"What was wrong with my old glasses, Mma? Why did they need improvement?"

"There was nothing wrong with them," said Mma Ramotswe hurriedly. "They were very fine glasses. It's just that these new ones are even finer." She repeated, even more emphatically, "Even finer, Mma."

Mma Makutsi seemed appeased. She looked at her watch, and Mma Ramotswe noticed that she was peering at it more closely than usual. Perhaps it was the light, as the sun had just gone behind a cloud and it was darker in the office than it had been a few minutes earlier.

"I think it is time for tea, Mma," she said. "I shall make it."

She got up from her desk and crossed over to where the kettle was perched on top of the filing cabinet. As she pressed the switch, she said to Mma Ramotswe, "Have your new neighbours moved in now, Mma?"

Mma Ramotswe nodded. "They have, Mma. I watched their furniture arrive this morning. It was very interesting, Mma."

And it had been, because there are few things more interesting in neighbourhood life than to witness the unpacking and the installation of one's neighbours' effects. People can say all sorts of things about themselves, can portray themselves in all sorts of false lights should they choose to do so, but their furniture is incapable of lying. Your furniture always tells the truth about you, and if the furniture is unvarnished, then so too is that truth.

The furniture van, a lumbering pantechnicon, had pulled up outside the neighbour's house at seven in the morning, at a time when Mma Ramotswe had just served breakfast to Motholeli and Puso. Mr J. L. B. Matekoni always breakfasted early, and he had already driven off in his truck to Tlokweng Road Speedy Motors. An early departure meant that he would beat the morning traffic, which, as was happening everywhere else, was getting worse and worse. Gaborone had grown, and its traffic problem had grown with it, although it was by nowhere near as bad as it was in many other cities. They had discussed that over morning tea in the office a few days earlier, a discussion that had led to a spirited exchange between Charlie, the junior assistant detective and part-time mechanic, and Mma Makutsi. Mma Makutsi had introduced the topic by mentioning the traffic jams that could now be encountered in Nairobi.

"I've heard that there are people who live in their cars these days," she said. "It takes so long to drive into work that they don't bother to drive back. They just pull in to the side of the road, change into their pyjamas, and sleep in the car. Then they reverse back to the office the next morning."

Charlie had laughed. "You cannot live in a car," he said. "Where would you cook your meals? Where would you go to the bathroom? Those are very important questions, Mma Makutsi."

Mma Makutsi had dismissed these objections. "I'm not saying that I have seen people doing these things, Charlie. I'm simply telling you what I have read in the newspaper — or it might have been a magazine. Somewhere I read it. They called them the 'car people'. That is what they said. They said they take their food with them. They did not say anything about the bathroom."

Mma Ramotswe had expressed the view that it would help if the government spent more on public transport. "We need more buses," she said. "We need more of these big buses that take a whole lot of people. One hundred people, sometimes, all in one bus."

"The government says it has no money," said Mma Makutsi. "They say it is not their job to buy these buses." She paused. "Anyway, even if we had more buses, there are still too many cars. Too many people are buying cars and then driving them round. What can you expect but traffic jams if people have too many cars?"

Charlie frowned. "So what do we do?"

Mma Makutsi had the answer. "We take cars away from people. The government should say: there are too many cars, and so you cannot have a car any longer. They would give them compensation, of course, but they would take their cars away."

"Whose cars?" challenged Charlie.

"People's," said Mma Makutsi.

"Including yours?" Charlie asked Mma Makutsi. "And Mma Ramotswe's white van? What about that? Should the government take Mma Ramotswe's van away from her?"

Mma Makutsi made a dismissive gesture. "Of course not, Charlie. I'm not suggesting that anybody should take Mma Ramotswe's van from her. She needs it to get into work."

"Ha!" crowed Charlie. "And your car, Mma Makutsi? You have that red car of yours with its big exhaust pipe. Think of all the smoke you make, Mma Makutsi, racing round in that red car. Think of that. And Phuti Radiphuti, too. He has a car with a big engine — I've serviced that engine and so I should know. It is a very thirsty engine, I can tell you. Think of the Limpopo in full flood, and that is how much petrol goes into that engine. Ow!"

Mma Makutsi glared at the young man. "You're talking nonsense, Charlie. Nobody is going to take my car. I need it to get into work and Phuti uses his car for his furniture business. Our cars would be . . ."

"Exempt?" offered Mma Ramotswe.

"Yes," said Mma Makutsi. "That's the word: exempt."

Mma Ramotswe looked down at her desk. Everybody wanted to look after the world, but nobody wanted to give up anything they already had. Mma Makutsi was right when she said there were too many cars, but the business of reducing the number of cars would never be easy. That was particularly so in Africa, where so many people had never had the chance to own a car, and now, just as they were able to afford one, along came people who said they should not have one. And the same thing applied to beef, she thought. Many people had not been able to afford much meat in the past; now, when they could, people who had been eating meat for a long time said it was time for everybody to stop. There was something unfair in that, she thought, and yet we only had one world, and only one Botswana in that world, and we had to look after them both.

But now Mr J. L. B. Matekoni was off to the garage — in his truck, which was not particularly economical to run and not at all green, she suspected — and she had just fed the children, and at that moment the removal van happened to draw up outside the neighbours' house. In such circumstances all that one could do was to tell the children to hurry up and finish their breakfast and get ready for school. Puso, of course, could walk there, as the school was just round the corner, but Motholeli, who was in a wheelchair, could not. On occasion, Puso would push her to school, taking pride in helping his sister, but in this hot weather, with all the dust the heat seemed to bring, Mma Ramotswe preferred to take the chair in her van. She would do that this morning, she thought, and then return to the house so that she could keep an eye on what was going on next door.

She was back at the house after the school run just in time to see the men, who had been perched on the tailgate of the removal van, eating sandwiches, now roll up their sleeves and begin to unload the furniture. This was the interesting part — more interesting, perhaps, than the actual meeting of the new neighbours themselves, whom she had already spotted over the fence when they were viewing their intended purchase. She felt a thrill of excitement, but then, a moment or two later, she felt something quite different. This was doubt. Should she allow herself to take such an interest in the household possessions of her new neighbours, or was this no more than nosiness — the sort of thing that idle village people loved to do because they had nothing better with which to fill their time? The otherwise unoccupied took a great interest in what everybody else had and did. And then they went off and talked about it, sometimes stirring up feelings of jealousy amongst those whose lives were less exciting and less blessed with material goods. Envy was a real problem in

10

villages, where there were plenty of people ready to resent those who had more than they did. It was not an edifying characteristic, and if Botswana had any faults, then this was one of them. It did not help, and people who encouraged it should feel real shame.

She thought about this, and almost persuaded herself that she should turn away and drive off to work, leaving the removal men to do their heaving and carrying unobserved. But then she thought: no harm will be done if I watch, but do not tell anybody about anything I might see. She thought about this for a few moments, closing her eyes, the better to facilitate judgement. Decisions made with closed eyes were, Mma Ramotswe thought, often weightier, more balanced. And now she made up her mind: if she watched, but did not speak about, what was unfolding next door, it would be a perfectly acceptable compromise between natural curiosity and a decent respect for the privacy of others. Her decision made, she settled on her veranda, in a cool spot away from the slowly rising morning sun, with a cup of freshly brewed redbush tea to hand. In that position she watched as the drama of the arrival took place.

Mma Ramotswe watched as the kitchen effects emerged. There was a large fridge, of newish manufacture, which required three men to carry it in, and this was followed by a fancy-looking cooker. This required careful manhandling out of the van and lifting onto a sturdy-looking trolley. On this it was wheeled round to the back of the house from where various shouted instructions emerged as men manoeuvred it into the kitchen. Next came boxes of pots and pans, handles sticking out of splits in the cardboard, and several boxes given over, she thought, to current provisions, judging by the trail of flour that one of them left as it was carried in. Mma Ramotswe smiled at that. It would be a good clue for a detective, she thought, and could imagine what Clovis Andersen, author of *The Principles of Private Detection*, might write about that. *If you find a trail of flour, you can be reasonably sure that somebody has been making their way into or out of a kitchen.* Beyond that conclusion, of course, there would be little one could say.

It took a good hour for the kitchen furniture and equipment to be off loaded and installed. It was now time for Mma Ramotswe to go to work, but she was enjoying herself far too much to do that. There were one or two matters to be dealt with in the office that morning, though none of them was urgent. Mma Makutsi would be there and she could deal with any new business that arose — not that this was likely. For some reason it was a quiet time, and new clients were few and far between. It might be the weather, Mma Ramotswe thought: the heat had been building up steadily, and in hot conditions people tended to behave themselves. Suspected unfaithfulness, the bread and butter of any private detective agency, was seasonal: the hot weather seemed to inhibit it, while the cooler weather brought it on. Clovis Andersen said nothing about this in his book, but then he was used to a climate in which people had the energy to engage in affairs at any time of the year. Here, who could be bothered, in the heat, to flirt with anybody, let alone embark on something more serious?

Of course, temptation could strike at any time, and in any circumstances, and there would always be a trickle of enquiries, no matter what the season was. The previous day they had heard from a prospective client, a woman in Lobatse who had witnessed a small child running up to her husband in a shopping mall. The child had shouted "Daddy, Daddy" and flung his arms around her husband's legs. "Silly child," the husband had said. "He has mistaken me for his daddy." But he had been flustered — far more than one might expect an innocent person to be in such circumstances. The child had been retrieved by a young girl who was clearly a nanny, and had been dragged away protesting and still shouting, "Daddy!" Could the No. 1 Ladies' Detective Agency look into this matter? Of course they could, and Mma Makutsi had agreed to drive down to Lobatse the following week and interview the client about her concerns. "My husband is a good man," the woman had said, "but you know what men are like, Mma. They are not good all the time."

"The only men who are good all the time," Mma Makutsi had said, "are the saints, and they are all dead now, Mma."

Charlie, who had overheard this conversation in the office, had scowled. "You have no right to talk about men like that," he protested. "There are many men who are good all the time. Many, Mma."

"Name one," said Mma Makutsi, adding, "Apart from Mr J. L. B. Matekoni, of course. He is a very good man on a permanent basis."

Charlie tried a different tack. "And women? Are women always good, Mma?"

Mma Makutsi did not reply immediately. Mma Ramotswe, who was amused by this exchange, decided to keep out of it.

At last Mma Makutsi said, "Women are human, Charlie. That is well known." She glanced at Mma Ramotswe as she said this. "That is well known" was Mma Ramotswe's phrase — the clincher of any argument, the settler of any point of dispute. But there were occasions when Mma Makutsi employed it, although she always glanced at Mma Ramotswe as she did so, as if to confirm she had the licence to use it.

"So," said Charlie, "if they are human, then they will be just as bad as men. All humans are equal, I think. Isn't that what the Constitution of Botswana says?"

"This has nothing to do with the Constitution of Botswana, Charlie," snapped Mma Makutsi. "This is psychology, and there has never been any doubt that women have better psychology than men when it comes to . . ." She waved a hand in the air. ". . . when it comes to these things."

"What things, Mma?"

"To behaviour," said Mma Makutsi. "Women are always thinking of what is best for children, for instance. They think: what is going to make children strong and happy? What is going to make sure that there is food on the table? What is best for everybody? Those are the questions that women are always asking."

"And men?" Charlie demanded. "Do men not think about those things too?"

Mma Makutsi replied that men sometimes thought about those things, but they often acted impulsively because they were impatient. Or they acted without thinking because . . . well, they didn't think in the same way as women. They thought that something needed to be done, and they did it. They did not think about the consequences.

And that was where the discussion had ended, as the office telephone had rung with another call, and human psychology was left for another day. Now, on her veranda, watching the removal men, Mma Ramotswe thought about the exchange between Mma Makutsi and Charlie, and reflected on the fact that there could be discussions between two people where both were wrong. You might even embody that in one of Clovis Andersen's rules, she thought: *Do not think that in any case where there are two competing arguments one of them has to be right: both can be wrong.*

Her thoughts were disturbed by a shout from one of the removal men, who had stumbled while carrying a small table. The table had landed on his foot and he had shouted out in pain. One of the other men had laughed, calling out some comment about carelessness. Mma Ramotswe was concerned; the man was crouched down now, rubbing his foot, clearly in considerable pain. Instinctively she rose from her seat and made her way to her gate.

"Are you all right, Rra?" she asked.

He looked up. He was a man of about forty, with the lightish brown skin that suggested a touch of San blood somewhere in his ancestry. His shirt was soaked in sweat, under the armpits, along the chest, around the collar.

"I have hurt my foot a bit," he said. "But I think it will be all right, Mma."

He stood up now, wincing slightly as he tested his weight on his foot.

"I have some of that stuff you can rub on your foot," Mma Ramotswe said. "You know that green ointment? Zam-Buk? The one that is very good for bruises?"

He shook his head. "That is kind of you, Mma, but we must finish this load." He looked inside the van, and Mma Ramotswe followed his gaze. There were still a few items remaining — bedroom furniture, she noted. She saw a wardrobe, still tied to the side of the van's interior to prevent its toppling over; two chests of drawers; a standing mirror. And then there were the beds. She counted them. One, two, three, four.

The man was looking up at the sky. "When is it going to rain, Mma?"

Mma Ramotswe sighed. "I ask myself that every morning, Rra. I go out into my garden and I look at my beans and I think, when is it going to rain? And the beans are thinking that too, I believe."

The man laughed. "And the grass. And the cattle. And the snakes down in their holes. They are coughing, I think, because of all the dust — the snakes are coughing."

16

Mma Ramotswe smiled. "That is a very odd thought, Rra. I can imagine a snake would have a long cough — a very long cough."

She looked into the van again. One of the other men was untying the beds, making them ready for removal. Four beds. Four single beds.

On impulse she asked, "Are there only four beds, Rra?"

He glanced into the van. "Yes, there are four. We loaded four, and we shall be unloading four. That is how it works, Mma."

She thought, *single* beds. She looked at the man. "No double bed," she muttered.

The comment had not been addressed to him, but he answered. "We do not ask about these things, Mma. We are removal men. You give us the furniture; we put it in the van; we drive wherever: one hundred kilometres, two hundred, one thousand if you want to go and live up in Zambia. We will take your things anywhere."

He looked at her, and then said, "We do not think about these things, Mma — not in our job."

She lowered her eyes, chastened. She felt that she wanted to tell him that she was not a gossip, that she was not one of those people who pried into the affairs of others. She wanted to explain to him that she was a detective and that it had become second nature to her to look at the world and then wonder what lay behind the things one saw. But she did not say any of this, because she felt ashamed, and he had his work to do, and she should leave them to it now.

He thanked her for the offer of the ointment and returned to his work. She went back to her veranda, where she finished her cup of redbush tea, and prepared to drive into the office. No double bed, she thought. And this was followed by the thought: this is not my business. It was important to think that particular thought, she reminded herself as she drove off towards the Tlokweng Road and the premises of the No. 1 Ladies' Detective Agency. There are things in this world that are one's business, and things that are not. It was sometimes a challenge to find exactly where the boundary between these two lay, and to act accordingly. That was the challenge. Yet here it was obvious: whether or not one's new neighbours slept in a double bed was no business of anybody but themselves. Others should not even think about it. So she told herself not to think about it, which of course is the surest way of guaranteeing that you will think about exactly the thing you do not wish to think about.

CHAPTER
TWO

Late People Talk to Us

Mma Makutsi had not been idle. "Since you are so late this morning, Mma Ramotswe," she said, "I have used the time to go through old files. I have taken out ones that we can get rid of now, I think."

Mma Ramotswe crossed the office and deposited on her shelf her bag and the keys to her van on her desk. Glancing at Mma Makutsi's desk she saw a pile of brown manila files, papers protruding here and there from between the covers. The sight made her think of the hours of work that each of these represented, and also of what lay behind each and every folder: the human emotions, the plans, the disappointments — and, in some cases at least, the triumphs. One or two of them, she noticed, had a familiar large red sticker on the outside denoting *Payment of Final Bill Pending*. That was a forlorn hope, now, she thought. And then there were the green stickers — not many — that signified *More Developments Possible*. Again, that was unlikely, Mma Ramotswe told herself. She tried to think of recent developments in any of these old cases, and could think of none. Perhaps a rewording of the sticker might be called for: *More*

Developments Possible, but Unlikely would be more realistic, she felt.

"You have been very busy, Mma," she said.

Mma Makutsi studied her fingernails in a vaguely prim manner. "Well, I thought that it would be a good idea to tackle something that we've been talking about for some time now." She paused, looking up from her fingernails. "Talking about, yes, but not getting done."

Mma Ramotswe was not sure whether there was a note of reproach in Mma Makutsi's voice. It was true that they had been planning to go through the filing cabinet in order to weed out dormant files, and on one or two occasions had almost embarked upon the task, only to be interrupted by the arrival of a client or the ringing of the telephone. There were other routine administrative tasks that needed to be tackled but that had been put off for one reason or another; this one, though, was more pressing than the others as the filing cabinet was now almost full and more recent files had been stacked, in no particular order, on a shelf next to the well-thumbed copy of Clovis Andersen's *The Principles of Private Detection*.

Mma Makutsi picked up one of the files. "This one, for example, Mma. Remember that man who ran the store and said his wife was having an affair? And then his wife came into the office and said the same thing about him? And we had to sit there with a straight face?"

Mma Ramotswe did remember, and she laughed at the recollection. "And then they both decided that it was a mistake and got back together."

There was more. Mma Makutsi lifted up the file and held it over the wastepaper bin. "And then they argued about who should pay the bill, and neither of them paid."

"I think we can throw that one away, Mma," said Mma Ramotswe. "Case closed."

The file fell into the bin. It was almost like an act of forgiveness, although there were no witnesses, save the two of them. Mma Ramotswe found herself raising her eyes briefly, almost guiltily, to the ceiling. At school in Mochudi, all those years ago — in that small school perched on top of the hill, with the village beneath it and the sound of cattle bells drifting up on the breeze; there, standing before the class, her teacher, the infinitely patient Mma Kenosi, had told them about the Recording Angel who noted down everything — "And I mean *everything*, boys and girls, that you do. So even if you do a good deed and nobody is there to witness it, that will be written down." And at that, she would raise her eyes heavenwards, and thirty-five pairs of eyes watching her would be raised in unison, as if in an orchestrated display. The habits of childhood, instilled by the Mma Kenosis of this life, may be overwritten by the demands of the years, but some vestiges remained — thoughts, ways of doing things, odd beliefs, superstitions . . . these things had a power over you that ensured their survival, even if it was in weakened form. And so it was that Mma Ramotswe thought briefly of the Recording Angel as Mma Makutsi tipped the defunct file into the bin. She had long since abandoned belief in such a person, because a moment's thought

21

was enough to explode the notion: how could anybody keep an eye on the millions — no, billions — of good, and bad, deeds that people did every day? Such a task was clearly impossible, even if you believed in angels, which she did not. Well, not *completely*: there were times when you *wanted* to believe in angels, and when you might just allow yourself a few moments of such a belief. When you were in danger, perhaps, you might secretly wish for angelic assistance, and might be forgiven for believing in something that you didn't believe in. Or when you wanted something so badly — that a grievously ill friend might be relieved of her suffering, one way or another, for example; then you might clutch at such a belief. And when your silent prayer was answered, was it not tempting to think that an angel had brought about that which you wanted? Was this not just an ordinary human way of thinking — or hoping, perhaps?

As she thought of this, she remembered the loss of her old friend, Charity, who had been a friend, too, of Mma Potokwani. Together, she and the matron of the Orphan Farm had spent the last two days of Charity's life nursing her through the cruel blows that her illness brought; the struggles for breath, the relentless coughing that racked her frail system. They had watched as their friend became thinner and thinner until there seemed so little of her, far too little to survive another night. But she had, and then, in the morning, as the sun rose over the acacia trees, she had suddenly become still and Mma Potokwani had turned to her and said, "That is the angel that has come for

22

her, Mma." And Mma Ramotswe, through her tears, had simply nodded, and kissed her late friend's brow. Then she had gone outside, because Mma Potokwani, who had been a nurse before she became a matron, knew what was required as a last service to those who have become late, and would do what was needed in private. The husband was there in the garden, watering the melons, and she saw from his eyes that he knew the news that she was bringing him from the sick room. And she said to him the first thing that came to her mind, which was, "An angel has visited this house, Rra." And that somehow made it easier for both of them; and so she had decided that even if there were no angels, we might still wish to believe in them because that made our life more bearable, and she was not ashamed to think like that.

Mma Makutsi brought her back to the present. "I saw them, by the way," she said, gesturing towards the freshly abandoned file. "They came into Phuti's store. They were looking for a new table. They seemed very happy. They were both laughing."

"I'm glad it all ended well for them," said Mma Ramotswe. And she was: she believed there came a time when debts had to be forgiven — and that applied to countries as well as people, she felt. There were some countries in Africa that were still paying for the spending sprees of their early post-independence rulers. It was not the fault of today's children, but then the world was a hard place and there always seemed to come a time when the wells of generosity ran dry.

Mma Makutsi grinned. "They saw me, you know. They saw me in the furniture shop. I was standing there with Phuti, and they saw me."

Mma Ramotswe raised an eyebrow. "And what happened, Mma?"

"They ran," Mma Makutsi replied. "He ran first, and then she ran after him. Phuti was very surprised. He asked me what was going on and I told him. He shook his head. He has problems with bad debts too."

"It is sometimes not easy to forgive," observed Mma Ramotswe.

"It's like stealing," said Mma Makutsi. "If you don't pay what you owe, it's like stealing. I am not so quick to forgive as you are, Mma Ramotswe." She leaned over to retrieve the file. "In fact, I am going to write to these people again and tell them I have not forgotten the bill."

Mma Ramotswe sighed. "You could try, Mma. But what about asking for half?"

"Ninety-seven per cent," said Mma Makutsi firmly. "I will ask them for ninety-seven per cent of what they owe. That will give them a three per cent discount."

They spent the next half-hour looking at some of the other files. It was slow work. With the day's quota of generosity expended, the remaining unpaid bill files were retained by Mma Makutsi for what she described as "one last push", while others, cases in which they had either solved the client's problem or been unable to help, were one by one disposed of and dropped into the wastepaper bin and an overflow cardboard box

24

retrieved by Mma Makutsi from the small storeroom at the back of the garage.

Now it was time for mid-morning tea. "One last word on these unpaid bills," Mma Makutsi said. "When I lived up in Bobonong, there was a man who had a little business selling stock food. You know those cattle licks, Mma — the ones with salt and this and that? You know those ones?"

Mma Ramotswe did know them. She was, after all, the daughter of the late Obed Ramotswe, fine judge of cattle, whose large herd had, after his death, provided her with the means to buy her house and start her business. She had absorbed a great deal of knowledge about cattle from her father, and knew what it was that cattle needed. He had said to her, "Cattle, Precious, will eat anything if they don't get the salt they need. You don't want your cattle to eat sticks and stones, do you? Or dirt? That is why they must have their licks." And then he had talked about potassium and zinc and vitamin D, and she had remembered some of these, but not all. She had remembered about magnesium, though, and the way he had spoken about the risk of the disease he called staggers if the cattle did not get the magnesium they needed.

She heard his voice again, as she heard it in her head now and then, at unexpected moments. Late people talk to us, she thought; they talk to us, but most of the time we are not listening because we are so busy with what we are doing here and now and there are so many problems to be dealt with. But then, when we stop for a moment and catch our breath, we might just hear the voices of the late people who love us, and they are whispering to us, quietly, like the wind that moves across the dry grass; and we know that it is them, although we also know that it cannot be them, for they are late. And so we try hard to hear, just to be sure, and their voices fade away and there is nothing once again.

Now it was Mma Makutsi talking, and she was telling her about the man in Bobonong who sold salt licks for people's cattle. "He let people buy them on account," she said. "If people did not have the money to pay, he would never send them away. Because that would mean their cattle would not get the salt they needed and you would never want to be responsible for another person's cattle dying. So he let them buy on credit and pay later. But . . ."

"Not everybody paid?" suggested Mma Ramotswe.

"That's right. Not everybody paid. But this man — the salt-lick trader — he had a very good way of getting them to pay, Mma. It always worked. One hundred per cent of the time — it worked."

Mma Ramotswe waited for the secret to be revealed. Was Mma Makutsi going to use a special Bobonong way of getting the agency's debtors to pay up?

"He used witchcraft," said Mma Makutsi. "He found this old witch doctor — you know, a *sangoma* — and he paid him a few pula to put a curse on the people who didn't pay their bills. Then he told them, and they all paid up very smartly — the next day, in fact. It was very effective."

Mma Ramotswe shot a disapproving look across the room. "But you're not going to do that, are you, Mma Makutsi?"

There was a note of disappointment in Mma Makutsi's answer. "No, Mma, I shall not do that."

Mma Makutsi got up to start making the tea. She had just switched on the kettle when the door opened and Mr J. L. B.

Matekoni, who had been inspecting a car in the garage workshop, came into the office, wiping the grease off his hands with a piece of the blue paper he kept for this purpose.

"There is a woman," he said to Mma Ramotswe. "There's a woman outside to see you, Mma."

Mma Ramotswe glanced at her diary. "We don't have anybody booked in, do we Mma?"

Mma Makutsi shook her head. "There is nobody."

"I'm not sure if she's a client," said Mr J. L. B. Matekoni. "She said it's personal. I told her to come and knock on the door. I told her that the garage was a separate business, but she seemed very shy. She wanted me to speak to you first — to find out whether you would see her."

"Show her in, Rra," said Mma Makutsi. "I will make an extra cup of tea for this timid lady."

Mr J. L. B. Matekoni finished wiping his hands. "She said she is a cousin."

Mma Makutsi spun round. "Of mine, Rra?"

"No." He looked across the room towards his wife. "Of Mma Ramotswe's."

Mma Ramotswe frowned. "Did you recognise her, Rra?"

Mr J. L. B. Matekoni was uncertain. "No, not really. Well, maybe slightly. She looked a little bit familiar, but not really."

"Well, that's clear enough," said Mma Makutsi.

Mma Ramotswe looked disapprovingly at Mma Makutsi. Then, turning to Mr J. L. B. Matekoni, she said, "I think you should bring her in, Rra."

Blessing Mompati sat in the client's chair directly opposite Mma Ramotswe, holding a mug of tea across which she blew a cooling breath.

"This tea is very hot," she said. "I am not complaining, Mma — it is very welcome, but it is hot."

"It will cool, Mma," said Mma Ramotswe. "And we are in no hurry. There is plenty of time to drink tea."

Blessing put the tea down on Mma Ramotswe's desk. "I have been trying to cut down on sugar." She had asked for three spoons. "But it is not easy, Mma."

From behind her, Mma Makutsi said, "It is a question of willpower, Mma."

Blessing half turned to answer Mma Makutsi. "I do not have much of that, Mma. Maybe that is my problem."

"I'm sure you do," said Mma Ramotswe.

Blessing shook her head. "I do not think so, Mma. It is the same thing with fat cakes. I know we shouldn't eat too many, but when I see a plate piled high with fat cakes, well —"

"Willpower again," interjected Mma Makutsi. "Sugar, fat cakes, cigarettes — it is all the same thing. Willpower."

Blessing spoke over her shoulder. "You must be very strong, Mma. Not all of us are strong."

Mma Ramotswe took control. "When you came in, Mma, it was a moment or two before I remembered who you are. I'm sorry if I looked blank. You should not look blank when a cousin comes to see you — even a distant cousin."

Blessing assured her that no offence had been taken. "We have not seen one another since we were girls, Mma. That is a long time ago."

"Many, many years," said Mma Ramotswe.

"I think we came to see you in Mochudi on our way down from Francistown. I remember your father."

"He is late now."

"I knew that. I'm very sorry. All the best people are late, Mma — or that's sometimes how it seems."

Mma Ramotswe took a sip of her tea. "The tea is cooler now, I think, Mma."

Blessing tested it, and agreed. "It is good to see you with your own business now, Mma," she said. "That man out there — the mechanic — is he the man you married?"

Mma Ramotswe nodded. "That's Mr J. L. B. Matekoni. He's my husband."

"I've heard that he is a very kind man," said Blessing. "That's what they say, anyway."

"He is. He's a good man. I am very happy with him."

A wistful look passed over Blessing's face. "I was not so lucky. I was with a man who drank. He was always drinking — all the time."

"There is no cure for that," said Mma Makutsi. "If men are drinkers, then that is what they are."

"Oh, I don't know," Mma Ramotswe said. "They can join these groups they have. There is one in that church near the stadium. They sing hymns. If you are tempted to have a drink, you can call them and they will send two or three people round to sing hymns with you until the need to drink passes. They say that it works."

"It is too late for him," said Blessing. "He fell into a ditch. You know, Mma, that is what they say about these people. They say that it is only when they end up down in the dirt that they will do anything about their problem."

"And did he?" asked Mma Makutsi. "Did he go to these people near the stadium?"

Blessing shook her head. "It was the rainy season, Mma. The ditch was full of water."

They fell silent. Mma Ramotswe caught Blessing's eye and then looked away. "I am very sorry, Mma."

"He is late, Mma?" Mma Makutsi asked — a little insensitively, thought Mma Ramotswe.

"He is late," said Blessing. "He fell into the ditch at night-time. He walked into it. The police said they thought it was about midnight. Somebody found him on the way to work the next morning. The water had drained out of the ditch, and so they wondered how you could drown in a ditch with no water. The police doctor said he had definitely drowned."

"I am very sorry to hear all this, Mma," said Mma Ramotswe.

"Thank you, Mma. It is some years ago, now. I am over it, I think."

"And you didn't meet anybody else?" asked Mma Ramotswe.

Blessing shook her head. "It is not easy, Mma. There are not many men these days. I don't know what has happened to the men."

This brought a reaction from Mma Makutsi, who snorted. "Men? Where are all the men? Good question, Mma — very good question."

Blessing turned round to face Mma Makutsi. "Well, Mma. Do you know the answer to that?"

"I do not," said Mma Makutsi. "But I have some ideas. I think that women have let men get away. They have let them run off. In the old days, women made men marry them because if they did not marry them, then they would not let the men kiss and cuddle them — if you know what I mean, Mma. They said: no kisses, no cuddles until you have bought the ring, spoken to the father and the uncles, and paid the lobola. Then there can be that sort of thing. But now? Kisses and cuddles straight away and then the men say, 'Thank you very much, Mma, but I am going away because there are all sorts of things that I would like to do — and getting married and settling down is not one of them.'" She paused. "That is what has happened, Mma."

"Possibly," said Mma Ramotswe. "Possibly, Mma."

"No, Mma Ramotswe," said Mma Makutsi. "Not possibly definitely. And then there are men who say that they do not like women. They say, 'I do not like ladies and so you can cross me off your list.' I am not making this up, Mma — that is what they say. And so they go off and that's the last any of us girls see of them, Mma, I can tell you."

Mma Ramotswe shifted in her seat. This was a difficult topic in Botswana society and people did not like to talk about it openly. Perhaps that was the trouble: if they talked about it, it would be different.

"I think the important thing is that people should be happy," she said. "There are some people who like one thing and others who like another. That is not something we should worry about too much. Why make people unhappy by saying they cannot be with the people they want to be with? Why, Mma?"

Mma Makutsi was tight-lipped. "I do not want anybody to be unhappy, Mma. I did not say that. I just said that some men have decided they do not like ladies, and so there are fewer men for the ladies who like men. That is all."

Mma Ramotswe decided to bring the conversation back from these major issues of demography and marriage. Discussions of those subjects tended to get you nowhere, she felt, interesting though they might be. If you thought there were too many people — or too few — then talking about it did not change the number of people there were.

"I am very pleased to see you, Mma," she said to Blessing. "But I was wondering whether there was anything that I could do for you. You aren't in need of a private detective, are you?"

Blessing smiled. "I am not, Mma. No, I came to see you because there is something I need to talk to you about — and you are my cousin."

"I am happy to talk to you, Mma," said Mma Ramotswe. "I am listening right now. What do you need?"

"Money," said Blessing.

CHAPTER
THREE

Rule No. 1

That evening, Mma Ramotswe did not tell Mr J. L. B. Matekoni about Blessing's request. She had intended to do so over dinner, having made him his favourite stew of Botswana beef, and having served it with his favourite vegetable, pumpkin — moistened, of course, with a large pat of butter and covered in a rich gravy from the roasting tin in which the beef had been prepared. After that, all that was required was salt and pepper sprinkled on the top, and there was a meal that would keep anybody happy, from the President down to the humblest of men in his remote cattle post. Not that such distinctions were encouraged in Botswana, where everybody was equal, in theory at least: in practice, it was not hard to pick out those who had more beef and pumpkin than others, and were, perhaps, not quite as ready to share their beef and pumpkin as they might be. But although that was a troubling issue, and one that certainly worried Mma Ramotswe, she was not thinking of that as she and Mr J. L. B. Matekoni sat down to their meal and he, sniffing at the steamy aromas rising from his plate, asked, "Is there a luckier man in all Botswana, my Precious, than the one you see seated at this table? Is there?" And she had smiled, because she loved receiving compliments of that nature — and who does not? — before replying, "But is there a luckier woman in all Botswana — or maybe even in all Africa — than this woman *you* see seated at this table?"

That would have been a good time to broach the subject of Blessing's visit to the agency, but somehow she missed the moment, and the conversation veered off in another direction. Then, at the end of the meal, Mr J. L. B. Matekoni had yawned and announced that he was too tired to talk any longer because of the long day in the garage and the difficulties with a gearbox that had proved to be resistant to all reason. So it was not until the next morning, when she brought him a cup of tea in bed, that she felt able to raise the delicate issue of Blessing.

It was delicate because Mma Ramotswe knew that Mr J. L. B. Matekoni had his views on people who relied on distant family connections to get some sort of favour from others. In his view it was this idea of obligation that led to corruption, the canker that had held Africa back from achieving its full potential. Corruption was the devil, he said, that led countries rich in resources to the begging bowl. It had happened so many times in so many different places, but never in Botswana. "And why?" he asked. "Because Seretse Khama would not tolerate corruption — that is why." And he, the first President, that good man who spoke with all the authority that came from his origins in the first family of the Bamangwato people, had said that there should be no corruption in Botswana and that those who had power should wield it for the good of all rather than for the lining of their own pockets. And that had worked, when all about them, in Angola, and South Africa, and Zimbabwe, officials and politicians had taken their cut and slowly drained the blood from their economies. Some had become immensely rich, funded by stolen diamonds or the bribes paid for large construction contracts — there were hundreds of ways of taking money that should not belong to you — and honest men and women had suffered as a result.

"And how does this happen?" Mr J. L. B. Matekoni asked. "It happens because of that thing you boast about, Mma Ramotswe. It happens because one person can go to another and say: you are my cousin, or my cousin's cousin, or even my cousin's cousin's cousin, and this means that you must give me the job or the contract. And so this thing grows, and puts down deep roots, just like the mopipi tree, deep roots that go right down into the heart of a country. Deep, deep. And soon nobody can do anything about it, because everyone is doing it, and there are no honest people left, and that is what corruption is, Mma."

Yes, thought Mma Ramotswe, yes, but . . . And the but was a big one. She thought he was right about how some people took advantage of family connections to get the things they wanted; he might be right about that, but at the same time she would not want to see that tradition abandoned, because that would make Botswana just like anywhere else where people did not think they had to help others. You had to look after other people because if you did not, then the world was a cold and lonely place, a place where, if you stumbled, there would be no hand to pull you to your feet. So even if Mr J. L. B. Matekoni was right about how people had abused this idea of mutual reliance, she could not bring herself to reject it.

Now, as she sat on the edge of their bed, while he sipped the tea she had made him, she said, "That woman who came to see me yesterday, Rra. You remember her?"

He nodded. "What did she want, Mma?"

"She wasn't a client, you know."

He took a further sip of his tea. "I know. She said something about being a cousin. I meant to ask you about her, but that gearbox I was busy with . . ." He shook his head. Gearboxes were the cross he bore in life. He did not mind shock absorbers or fuel pumps, or brake drums, but gearboxes were another matter altogether.

"Her name is Blessing. She is a very distant cousin — you know how it is: daughter of a cousin who married a cousin — that sort of thing."

Mr J. L. B. Matekoni smiled. "That makes all of us cousins," he said. "You, me, Mma Makutsi — even Charlie, I suppose. We're all related."

"Yes, we are," said Mma Ramotswe. "And if you trace it far back enough, we all come from the same place — way, way back. East Africa. Even people up in Iceland — they come from East Africa originally. So everyone is a cousin."

"That is this DNA they talk about," said Mr J. L. B. Matekoni, adding, with mock seriousness, "I should like to see some of this stuff one day. I wonder if it looks like motor oil. High-grade motor oil, naturally."

She laughed. "We are not motor cars, Mr J. L. B. Matekoni. Well, I'm certainly not . . ."

He drank the last of his tea and put the empty cup down on his bedside table. Putting his hands behind his head to act as an extra pillow, he prepared to enjoy the last few moments in bed before getting up. He closed his eyes.

"You aren't going back to sleep, are you?" asked Mma Ramotswe. "It's a working day, remember."

His voice was drowsy. "I'm not going back to sleep. I'm just thinking."

"About?"

"About those early people back then — you know, the ones in East Africa — the ones whose skulls they dug up. I was thinking about them having a sort of *kgotla* meeting and saying, 'It's about time we got moving.'" He opened his eyes and smiled. "And then one of them says, 'How about going off to Europe or India? There will be big opportunities there.'"

"This Blessing," Mma Ramotswe persisted. "She came to tell me about one of our relatives. She says that he is not well."

Mr J. L. B. Matekoni sighed. "People are always falling ill, Mma. That is the way we are." He paused. "I'm sorry, of course, it is not very pleasant being unwell, but it is always happening, I'm afraid."

"And —"

He interrupted her. "And they need money? Right?"

38

Mma Ramotswe lowered her eyes. He knew how these things worked, just as she did. She gave a wordless reply, nodding to confirm what he had said.

Mr J. L. B. Matekoni sat up and began to get out of bed. "It's always the same, Mma. This one, that one — everyone needs money. There's never enough, no matter how careful you are, no matter how hard you work. There is always a need for more money."

"It is a man called Tefo Kgomo. He worked in the mines up at Selebi-Phikwe and is now living down here — just outside town. You get to his place from the Lobatse Road. Down that way."

Mr J. L. B. Matekoni donned a clean shirt. He gave another sigh. "And what is wrong with him, Mma?"

"His hips," she said. "He has arthritis in both his hips. It is very difficult for him to walk now. It is always very painful."

"Can't they do something? I thought that these days they have an operation."

"Yes," said Mma Ramotswe. "They do have an operation. They can put in new joints."

"It's amazing," said Mr J. L. B. Matekoni. "Just like cars, Mma, don't you think? A new set of engine valves. A new suspension system. Just like cars."

"You're right, Rra. It is amazing. But Tefo cannot get these things, she said."

Mr J. L. B. Matekoni paused in his dressing. "But there's that big hospital down in Lobatse. That's close to where he lives, surely. They have plenty of doctors there. My friend, Thomas, who has his garage down that way says that he looks after the cars of at least register works. Oh yes, they are very good at that, I can tell you!

"So," the client went on, "I am very happy to be bringing my vans to you, Rra, because I know that I will not have to take out a bank loan to pay your bill. I also know that you will try to fix anything that needs to be fixed rather than just giving up and throwing some part away. That is the difference."

"Thank you, Rra. It is good to hear that you approve of what we do at Tlokweng Road Speedy Motors."

Any relationship based on such sentiments can survive the occasional cancellation at short notice. In addition, Mr J. L. B. Matekoni knew that the calling-off of the service was for a very good reason: the client was required to provide sound amplification for a major funeral taking place out of town. This was for a well-respected retired politician who, as a young man, had served under Seretse Khama himself and who, full of years, had died out at his cattle post, on the land that he loved, amidst the cattle that he cherished. There would be large crowds at the ceremony in his village, and the speeches would be long. There was nothing worse than listening to a speech you could not hear, and the family was keen to have good loudspeaker arrangements to ensure that everybody could pick up every word of what was said.

The cancellation, justified though it was, left the garage idle. For this reason, when his eye fell on Mma Ramotswe and Mma Makutsi returning from their visit to Blessing, it occurred to Mr J. L. B. Matekoni to service the van and perhaps attend to the suspension.

Suspension was the van's main weak point — amongst rather a lot of weak points, if the truth be told — this being particularly so on Mma Ramotswe's side of the vehicle. "Your van sags a bit," he had said to her, "because the weight is mostly on one side, Mma . . ." And he had added quickly, "That is quite normal, of course. It is nothing to do with —"

"Being traditionally built?"

"No, it is nothing to do with that, Mma. It is a distribution issue. That is all."

Now he turned to Fanwell and suggested that he get the key from Mma Ramotswe and move her van onto the inspection ramp. "We can spend a bit of time on that front suspension," he said. "And the oil will need changing. Give an old engine clean oil and she'll thank you."

"Who'll thank you, Rra? Mma Ramotswe or the engine?"

Mr J. L. B. Matekoni smiled. "I meant the engine," he replied. "But Mma Ramotswe will thank you too."

Fanwell drove the van over and positioned it on the pneumatic ramp. As he got out of the cab, he remarked to Mr J. L. B. Matekoni, "Funny smell, Rra."

Mr J. L. B. Matekoni frowned. You had to watch the electrics on an old vehicle, as cables had a habit of burning out when their plastic sleeves rotted. "Something burning, do you think?"

Fanwell shook his head. "You stick your nose in there, boss. It's not that sort of smell. That plastic burning smell is different. I always recognise that. No, this is . . . Well, it's a sort of . . . sort of cattle smell." He frowned; something was puzzling him. "But not quite."

Mr J. L. B. Matekoni opened the driver's door and sniffed at the air inside. He looked puzzled as he walked round to the back of the van and lowered the tailgate. He sniffed inside the back of the van.

"It's coming from in there," he said. "And yet, it's empty. There's nothing in the van."

Fanwell scratched his head. "But you must admit that there has been *something*, boss. It's not there now, but there was something there earlier on. Has Mma Ramotswe been carting cattle dung around? Maybe for use in somebody's fire, do you think? Or for making one of those traditional floors?"

Mr J. L. B. Matekoni was at a loss. "Vehicles have a smell," he said to Fanwell. "We all know that. But this . . . I have never smelled a van that has *this* particular smell." He paused. "Perhaps I should ask Mma Ramotswe what she's been carrying in here. Sometimes she goes to that garden centre, to Sanitas, and gets those unusual fertilisers for her beans. Some of them smell a bit strange, if you ask me. But this smell . . ." He shook his head. "This is what I would call a mysterious smell, Fanwell."

Fanwell shrugged. "Or Charlie might know?"

"Why Charlie?" asked Mr J. L. B. Matekoni.

"Because he's been driving the van. Mma Ramotswe lent it to him. Did she not tell you?"

Mr J. L. B. Matekoni did not answer, but turned on his heel and made his way into the office to have a word with Mma Ramotswe. She was busy talking on the telephone, but signalled to Mr J. L. B. Matekoni to sit down in the client chair while she finished the call. Mma Makutsi was filing — an activity that always engaged her attention completely, and so she just nodded curtly and continued with her task.

"Well, Rra," said Mma Ramotswe as she put down the receiver. "Are you ready for a cup of tea?"

Mr J. L. B. Matekoni shook his head. "I'm about to change the engine oil in your van," he said. "And give it the once-over too."

She thanked him. She remembered what he had told her about the importance of regular oil changes in an old vehicle.

"But there is one thing," Mr J. L. B. Matekoni said. "One thing is puzzling me, Mma. And it's puzzling Fanwell too. There is a smell, you see. I was wondering what you had been carrying in the van."

For a few moments, Mma Ramotswe did not answer. But then she remembered; yes, there had been a smell, and she had noticed it the previous day, when she had been driving home. She had opened the window to try to get rid of it, but it had lingered. She had made a mental note to ask Mr J. L. B. Matekoni about it, but it had slipped her mind. Now she said, "Yes, Rra. You are absolutely right. There *is* a smell. I smelled it yesterday."

"And did you have anything in the van that might have caused it?"

She shook her head. There was always a reason for a smell. She did not think that Clovis Andersen had said anything about smells in *The Principles of Private*

Detection, but had he addressed the subject he would undoubtedly have said something like, *There is no smell without a reason for a smell. That is basic. Rotten smell, rotten situation* . . . Perhaps she could write that in the margin in the chapter on "Drawing conclusions from the evidence of your senses" — a very important chapter that she and Mma Makutsi had often discussed.

Mr J. L. B. Matekoni raised the question of Charlie's use of the van. "What did Charlie do with your van? Fanwell said that you lent it to him yesterday."

"He needed it to help a friend with something."

"With *something*?"

Mma Ramotswe shrugged. "Yes, Mr J. L. B. Matekoni. He did not tell me what it was. He was helping a friend to transport something."

Mma Makutsi now detached herself from her filing. She had warned Mma Ramotswe that Charlie might be up to something, and here was the fallout she had worried about. She fixed Mr J. L. B. Matekoni with a quizzical stare. "Has he done something to the van, Rra? This morning I thought there was something wrong with it." She threw a glance at Precious. "I said that, didn't I, Mma Ramotswe?"

"The van is all right," said Mr J. L. B. Matekoni. "It's just that there's a smell."

Mma Makutsi's eyes narrowed. "A smell, Rra? An illegal smell? Do you think it's an illegal smell?"

"I wouldn't say that," replied Mr J. L. B. Matekoni. "It's certainly not *dagga*. You can always tell if somebody's been smoking *dagga*. No, it's not that."

"But still illegal, do you think?" pressed Mma Makutsi.

She wanted him to say yes, it was, but he did not. And perhaps I should not be surprised, she thought; she would be hard pressed to think of any other illegal smells, although undoubtedly there were some. The smell of money being laundered, for example — that might be a memorable smell, if one were ever to encounter it, although of course nobody ever actually put dirty money in the wash . . .

"I'm not saying anything about illegality," said Mr J. L. B. Matekoni. "All I'm saying is that Charlie must have been carrying something unusual yesterday. Now there is a smell. And there is also a bit of buckling on the tailgate." He paused. "Where is Charlie, by the way?"

"It is his day off," said Mma Ramotswe.

"I'd like to have a word with him," said Mr J. L. B. Matekoni. "I'd like to ask him to explain himself. If you borrow somebody's vehicle, you don't abuse it."

He said that with conviction. But it was not only his deep-seated respect for vehicles that had been offended here; there was the additional issue of truth-telling. Mr J. L. B. Matekoni felt strongly about the truth — as did Mma Ramotswe — and the idea that somebody should fail to mention damage done to a borrowed item was anathema to him.

"He'll be at his uncle's place, where he used to stay," said Mma Makutsi. "He hangs about there on his day off. That new wife of his . . . Queenie-Queenie . . . She works, and so he can't see her until after five."

Charlie had recently married, and was living in a rented flat near the village, courtesy of his new father-in-law.

Mr J. L. B. Matekoni looked at Fanwell. "I think I'm going to go and have a word with him. You come too, Fanwell."

Fanwell looked uncomfortable. If Charlie was going to be berated — which looked likely — he was not sure that he wanted to be party to that. Charlie asked for this sort of thing to happen, but he and Fanwell had been through a lot together over the years, and there was an old bond between them.

"But there are things to do here," he began. And then, rather lamely, "Work and . . ." He trailed off.

Mr J. L. B. Matekoni's expression suggested the subject was closed: Fanwell would be accompanying him. He was a mild man, not given to strong views or displays of anger, but the young mechanic could tell that his boss was rattled.

"I'll come, boss," Fanwell said quickly, wiping his hands on a twist of the blue absorbent paper dispensed from a large roll on the wall. He looked down at the ground: he had warned Charlie that he would take matters too far one day — he had told him. Whatever could have possessed him to think that he could damage Mma Ramotswe's van, fail to mention what had happened, and then get away with it? As a very young man — an eighteen-year-old — Charlie had been able to get away with virtually anything through sheer charm. People forgave him because of his jaunty good looks and his winning smile. Those seemed to work with everybody — they were particularly effective with women; but men, too, seemed susceptible to them. It was a different effect with them, thought Fanwell: men saw in Charlie the boy they once were — or would have liked to be. Older women saw him as a wayward son — they wanted to mother him — while to young women he was seditiously attractive: a bad boy who wasn't quite as bad as all that, who would calm down once a wedding ring was placed on his finger and he was staked off as occupied territory.

Fanwell was not a risk-taker. When attending to car engines he tested nuts before he attempted to take them off the bolt; Charlie would use brute force, not caring about stripping the thread. When connecting a wire to a terminal, Fanwell would use a carefully positioned drop of solder, just to be sure, whereas Charlie would simply make a loop with the end of the wire and wind it round the screw. The difference was stability and permanence; Charlie's mechanical interventions might fix a problem, but they would do that only for a short while. Sooner or later the patch would be shaken off by the vibrations that pass through any car in motion, and the problem for which help had been sought would recur. "People don't like bringing their cars back to the garage," Mr J. L. B. Matekoni explained. "Mechanics are like dentists: people don't want to see them too often."

Charlie had raised a finger to make a point. "Me," he said, "I've never been to the dentist. Not once. Ever."

Mr J. L. B. Matekoni had ignored this, but Fanwell had expressed surprise. "Never? Never ever, Charlie? You mean you've never gone, even if he didn't do anything to your teeth?"

Charlie had struck a nonchalant pose. "Never. That's what I said. Why go to the dentist unless your teeth are sore. Mine aren't." He opened his mouth and tapped his front teeth. "These teeth — see them — they're never sore. Never. And all the teeth behind them are in first-class condition Al. I don't need a dentist to tell me that."

Fanwell shook his head. "Everyone needs to go to the dentist, Charlie. They told us that at school. Remember that science teacher who gave lessons on personal hygiene? Remember him? What did he say, Charlie? What did he say?"

Charlie shrugged. "He was always saying things. That's the trouble with teachers — they spend a lot of their time saying things. If they said fewer things — hardly anything — then people would listen to them. But they don't."

Fanwell looked to Mr J. L. B. Matekoni for support, which was forthcoming. "Fanwell is right. Things can be going on inside your teeth, Charlie. Outside, they can look fine, but once you get inside they can be full of rot." Mr J. L. B. Matekoni paused. "You should see a dentist, Charlie. I will pay for you to have a check-up."

Charlie was unconvinced. "That's good of you, boss. But I don't want to waste your money. If I went to a dentist he'd take one look and then say, 'First-class teeth — nothing needed there.' But we'd still have to pay, you see, and I don't want to waste your money, boss."

"But it's not just about teeth," Fanwell persisted. "There's something called gum disease, Charlie. If your guns get sick, then your teeth drop out. You wake up one morning and you have no teeth. That has happened many times. And if you had no teeth, what would the girls say?"

"They'd say, 'No thanks,'" offered Mr J. L. B. Matekoni. "Girls like a man to have teeth."

Charlie laughed. "How do you know that, boss? I don't want to be rude, but how do you know what girls want?"

Mr J. L. B. Matekoni took the question in a good-natured way. "I might surprise you, Charlie," he said. "You may not know that I was a big man with the women back in the old days. Oh yes, you can smile at that, but I was. There were always women watching me, waiting for their chance."

Even Fanwell was surprised. "You must have been very popular, Rra. What happened?"

Mr J. L. B. Matekoni looked hurt. "What happened? Are you saying that . . ." He made a helpless gesture.

Fanwell quickly apologised. "I did not mean that, Rra. I did not mean to say that you are not popular still. I think you are. Women are still watching you, Rra. I have seen it."

Mr J. L. B. Matekoni was suddenly interested. "Oh, really, Fanwell? Where are these women? I have not seen them, I'm afraid. I'm prepared to accept they are there, but I have not seen them myself."

Charlie caught Fanwell's eye. "You shouldn't be winding the boss up," he said. "There are no women, Rra. Or not that we have seen."

"There could be," said Fanwell. "You know what women are like, Charlie. They are always on the lookout for a better man. They look at the man they already have and think: there must be better men than this one. That's what I believe they think." He lowered his voice. "I have heard women say that — using those exact words. It is very shocking." He paused. "Even that Queenie-Queenie of yours. I don't want to make you feel insecure, Charlie, but how do you know what goes on in her head? How do you know that she isn't thinking: there must be men who are a bit better than Charlie? That's what I would be thinking if I were going out with you. That's what I'd be saying to myself."

They drove in Mr J. L. B. Matekoni's truck to the street in the heart of Old Naledi where Charlie's uncle's house occupied a corner lot. It was a shabby part of town, one of the cheapest suburbs, ignored by the wave of prosperity that had moved across so many other parts of Gaborone. Many of the houses here were not much more than shacks, even if there were none of the tarpaulin and tin shelters of the real shanty town. Such places had not come into existence in Botswana because the poverty that produced them had been kept at bay, but even so, there were still families who lived in cement-block houses of one room and a make-do kitchen, where people washed in small tin tubs, and where the characteristic odour of penury, that smell of

Mme Ramotswe nodded. She was an admirer of the Queen, who she thought was just like Mma Potokwani — one of those people who were single-minded in the performance of their duties. Such people just went on and on doing what was expected of them. The Queen went round opening things and shaking hands with people; Mma Potokwani spent her days chasing people up to support the orphans, to donate surplus food, to pass on children's clothes and trainers, to find jobs for the children once they were grown up and ready to leave school. She never took no for an answer; she never gave up.

And there was Prince Charles, who she knew loved Botswana. When he came again to visit the country, she would try to invite him for tea. He would be too busy to come, of course, and there were people around him who would fend off invitations, but she knew they would have a great deal to talk about: about the rains and the crops; about looking after the world; about remembering that when all was said and done we lived on the land and had to give the land the love that it needed if it was to continue to provide for us.

"It would be good to have two birthdays," said Mma Potokwani. "But I think we have to be content with one."

The kettle having boiled, she made the tea. Then, once that had been poured, a jug of milk was passed around. Mma Makutsi took no more than a dash of milk in hers, while Mma Ramotswe, who liked her tea milky — even when she was drinking her favourite redbush tea — poured a generous volume of milk into her cup.

And then there was sugar. Mma Makutsi hesitated, as if conscious of an invisible censor — her shoes, perhaps, who had once ticked her off for eating three fat cakes in a row — but then helped herself to a half-spoon, passing the sugar bowl on to Mma Ramotswe. She did not hold back from helping herself to one and a half spoons — but filled so generously as to be the equivalent of three more modest spoonfuls. Then the bowl was passed to Mma Potokwani, who took three and a half.

The cake was served by Mma Potokwani, who told her guests that there were more cherries than usual in the mixture. Cherries had been on promotion at the supermarket, she explained, and she had stocked up. "Children like cherries, you see, and I give them as a reward if a child does something especially good."

Mma Ramotswe smiled as she imagined a well-behaved child having a sticky and glistening cherry popped into its mouth by Mma Potokwani. "Perhaps the government could do that too," she mused. "Not for children, but for adults. There could be special ceremonies at which people who have done good things would line up to get a cherry from one of the government ministers."

Mma Makutsi chuckled. "That's a very good idea, Mma. That nurse — Sister Banjule — you remember her? She would be at the top of the list."

Mma Ramotswe nodded. Sister Banjule, who ran the Anglican Hospice, would be a very good candidate for this reward. She had looked after so many people at the end of their days, and done so with kindness — the greatest compliment anybody could pay a nurse or a doctor. Kindness. It was not a complicated thing, kindness — we all knew how to be kind, and we all recognised it when we came across it. Sister Banjule had looked after Mma Makutsi's late brother, Richard, when he had died. His life had not been of much importance or significance to others — he was a very ordinary man, who had not really done very much — but she had made him feel cherished in those final few days, and Mma Makutsi had never forgotten that.

"Yes," said Mma Ramotswe. "She would be at the top of the list — right up at the top of the list, Mma Makutsi." She looked at Mma Potokwani. She was another person who should be given a cherry by the government, but Mma Ramotswe would not mention that now, as Mma Potokwani was modest and expected no reward.

They bit into their cake. The taste of cherries, liberally sprinkled through the dried fruit that made up much of the cake's bulk, came through strongly. Mma Makutsi closed her eyes in a transport of delight. "This is very fine cake, Mma," she said to Mma Potokwani.

"I am in complete agreement with Mma Makutsi," said Mma Ramotswe.

"I am very happy," said Mma Potokwani, taking a sip of her tea. "It would be a different matter if I had guests who did not like cherries."

The conversation moved on. "There is something we need to tell you about," said Mma Ramotswe. "It is a

139

very strange thing. You will not have heard of something like this, I think."

Mma Potokwani grinned. "You cannot shock me, Mma Ramotswe — if that is what you are worried about. Remember I am a matron — with hospital training — and if you are a matron you have usually seen everything." She paused, to shake her head, as if remembering some of the more shocking things she had seen in her career. "No, I am never surprised to hear what people get up to — especially men."

Mma Makutsi agreed with that. "Especially men," she said.

"And sometimes ladies, surely," said Mma Ramotswe. "We must not be too hard on men."

"That's true," said Mma Potokwani. "Ladies are not always as innocent as they appear. For instance . . ."

She did not need to finish. All three of them were thinking of the same person, and there was no need to spell out the name. Violet Sephotho.

"But let's not worry too much about all that," said Mma Potokwani eventually. "You were about to tell me, Mma Ramotswe, of some shocking thing. Well, I am listening now."

"It has nothing to do with Violet," Mma Makutsi said. "I could tell you some shocking things about her, Mma Potokwani, but . . ."

Mma Ramotswe shared her reservation. "We could do that some other day, perhaps. We would not want to burden Mma Potokwani unduly."

Mma Potokwani protested that she was perfectly happy to be burdened with disclosures about Violet

Sephotho. She was by no means a gossip, but she enjoyed a scandalous story as much as the next person, and when you lived out at Tlokweng you sometimes felt that you were missing out on some of the juicier goings-on in Gaborone itself. Not that Gaborone was a hotbed of such things, but a large town inevitably had a spicier life than a small town, and those who lived in small towns, or in the country, might be forgiven for taking an interest in what their urban cousins were getting up to.

"Well," said Mma Makutsi, "as I was telling Mma Ramotswe only recently, when she was at the Botswana Secretarial College — at the same time that I was there, Mma —"

"And where you got ninety-seven per cent, if I'm not mistaken," interjected Mma Potokwani.

Mma Makutsi inclined her head. "Yes, that was indeed the case, Mma, but what I was going to mention was the fact that Violet had three —"

Mma Ramotswe interrupted her. "I really think we should talk about that some other time. I really do."

"— boyfriends," Mma Makutsi finished.

"Three boyfriends!" exclaimed Mma Potokwani.

"A morning boyfriend, an —"

Mma Ramotswe cleared her throat. "The thing that we came to tell you about, Mma Potokwani, concerns Charlie."

Mma Potokwani seemed disappointed to be leaving the subject of multiple boyfriends, but now gave Mma Ramotswe her full attention. "Ah, Charlie," she sighed.

"He is always getting himself into difficulties. So, what's it now, Mma Ramotswe? More girl trouble?"

"He is not having girl trouble at present," interjected Mma Makutsi. "That is a thing of the past, now. He went off and got married. He did it very quietly."

Mma Potokwani approved. "That will be very good," she said. "It is always the best thing for a young man like Charlie. If a young man finds a nice girl, then everything works out well. I have seen that time and time again with the boys here. When they grow up and make their own lives, I watch the ones who had a bad start and who may have been a bit difficult. I watch them, and see what happens. If they come back with a nice girl to introduce to me, then I know straight away that everything will be fine. That will go for Charlie too, I think."

"I hope so," said Mma Ramotswe. "But at the moment there is a more pressing matter. Charlie has been looking after an animal that I'm afraid is going to cause problems for him."

Mma Potokwani shook her head. "Don't tell me, Mma Ramotswe. A dog. I've seen young people do that. They get a puppy and they forget that having a puppy is like having a baby. It's almost as much work. And then the puppy gets bigger and bigger and some of them are badly behaved and start biting people, and then there is all sorts of fuss. And the poor dog gets kicked out and ends up wandering around until it's run over or a leopard eats it or something like that."

"Leopards like to eat dogs," said Mma Makutsi. "And so do crocodiles. Phuti knew a man who had a boy hunting dog called Simba. He was a very strong dog, that one, who had jaws like a hyena. Have you seen hyena jaws, Mma Potokwani? They are very big and powerful. You do not want them to bite you if you can avoid it."

Mma Ramotswe began to steer the conversation back to Charlie, but Mma Makutsi was determined to continue her story. "This dog," she went on, "went with its owner down to the Limpopo one day. He was looking for guinea fowl, I think, because they have them in the bush out there. Anyway, he decided to walk down to the edge of the river to see what was going on down there, and there were some flat rocks that stretched out into the water. There was quite a lot of water, as there had been good rains and the Limpopo was in flood."

Mma Potokwani winced. "You have to be careful, you know. That river can be dangerous."

"Yes," said Mma Makutsi. "It can. But this man — this friend of Phuti's — was not careful. He walked out onto those flat rocks and his dog followed him — this horrible big dog called Simba. And since he was thirsty, the dog put his head down to drink some water from the river, and that was when it happened. Right in front of that man, a crocodile suddenly came up out of the water, grabbed the dog by the nose, and pulled him into the river. There was a lot of splashing, and the man threw some rocks into the water where the crocodile had disappeared with the dog, but there's not much you can do, Mma Potokwani, if a crocodile has you by the nose. They do the death roll, you see. Phuti told me about it. The crocodile spins his prey round and round underwater and he drowns him. That is what happens, Mma."

There was a short silence as they contemplated the fate of the dog. Then Mma Ramotswe said, "It's not a dog in Charlie's case, Mma Potokwani. It's an elephant. Charlie has got hold of a baby elephant."

Mma Potokwani's eyes widened, and then she let out a whoop of astonishment. "An elephant, Mma? A baby elephant? Oh, that is very funny." Tears of mirth began to show in her eyes; she wiped them away. "That is the funniest thing I have heard for many years. An elephant!"

Mma Ramotswe was taken aback by her friend's reaction. The fact that Charlie had ended up with an elephant was, in a sense, amusing — but not *that* amusing. She tried, as gently as she could, to impress on Mma Potokwani the gravity of the situation — a difficult task in any circumstances, as Mma Potokwani's nature was one of breezy confidence. "It's tethered to a post on wasteland behind his uncle's place," she said. "He's tied it to a metal post in the ground. That's all. There are no fences, Mma. No stockade."

Mma Potokwani shook her head in continued disbelief. "An elephant. Would you believe it, Mma Ramotswe? Mma Makutsi, would *you* believe it? Had you said, 'Charlie has a puppy,' I wouldn't have been all that surprised. But an elephant, ladies — an elephant!"

"You can't keep an elephant like that," Mma Ramotswe continued.

144

Mma Potokwani laughed again. "You can't keep an elephant at all," she said. "No, an elephant is not a chicken or a duck. It is not a goat."

Mma Makutsi rolled her eyes. "It is definitely not, Mma. But I don't think anybody thought it was. Nobody has been saying, 'An elephant is just like a goat.' Nobody, Mma."

Mma Potokwani smiled at this contribution, before continuing, "Oh, Mma Ramotswe, I thought I'd heard everything until I heard this. An elephant!"

"It's dangerous," said Mma Ramotswe simply. "Very dangerous."

"You don't need to tell me that," agreed Mma Potokwani. "Did you read in the newspaper about that poor person up north? That late person?"

Mma Ramotswe shook her head. The *Botswana Daily News* was full of unfortunate things that befell people. And these things were inevitable, given the nature of the world and the things that could go wrong. But you couldn't let all that deter you, she thought. You soldiered on; you carried on doing what you thought was the right thing to do; you soldiered on.

"Well," continued Mma Potokwani, "there was a report from up your way, Mma Makutsi — not Bobonong itself, but a bit further west, past the Makgadikgadi Pans. Up there in the middle of nowhere." She paused. A discouraging look from Mma Makutsi warned her that she was on tricky ground. And so she added, quickly, "I'm not saying that Bobonong is in the middle of nowhere, Mma Makutsi. I'm not saying that. Bobonong is an important place because . . ."

She had gone too far. Had she stopped immediately after admitting the importance of Bobonong, there would have been no difficulty, but she had unwisely started to explain why this should be so, and she realised she had not the slightest idea what happened in Bobonong.

Mma Makutsi smiled. "You're right, Mma. There is a lot going on in Bobonong. What were you thinking of in particular, Mma?"

"Oh, it's difficult to say," said Mma Potokwani. "These places, you know what they're like. There's always something." She paused. "But let's not worry about Bobonong. I wanted to tell you about what happened in this other place — the one I was talking about. You see, an elephant walked into a village and knocked down this poor man's hut. He was sheltering inside it because he had heard the elephant, but its walls were made of straw and mud and the elephant just had to lean on them to knock it down. The poor man had no chance."

"That's very sad, Mma," said Mma Ramotswe. "Imagine what it is like to have your house knocked over by an elephant."

Mma Makutsi had views on that. "It's because people are building their places on elephants' land," she said. "If you leave elephants alone, they'll leave you alone. They have their own places, and all you have to do is keep away from those and you'll be all right."

"But there isn't enough land," said Mma Ramotswe. "That's the problem, isn't it? There are too many people and many of them want to plant crops in places where the elephants live. So the elephants think: these people are on our land, and they rush round and knock things over and frighten everybody because they're so big and so powerful. And then somebody takes a shot at an elephant and all the elephants feel very strongly about that and begin to eat vegetables from people's gardens and frighten everybody. And then you have a big incident."

Having delivered her views on the subject, Mma Ramotswe sighed. Mma Potokwani, the attentive hostess, interpreted this as a coded request for a further slice of fruit cake. Reaching for the cake tin, she cut a large slice and tipped it onto Mma Ramotswe's plate. Then she did the same for Mma Makutsi.

"Mma Potokwani," said Mma Ramotswe. "You will be responsible for my needing a new wardrobe — all my dresses . . ."

"That is just shrinkage," said Mma Potokwani. "People blame cake for that sort of thing, but they forget that dresses have a natural tendency to shrink with age."

Mma Makutsi laughed. "Phuti's trousers have been shrinking for a long time. He is always complaining about that."

Mma Ramotswe took a bite of her fruit cake and then washed it down with a swig of tea. "This elephant," she said, "this elephant of Charlie's — you know what I am worried about, Mma Potokwani? I am worried about the children."

Mma Potokwani frowned. "The children, Mma? What children?"

Mma Ramotswe looked out of the window. It was a cunning tactic, and it was working — just as Clovis Andersen said it would. He said somewhere in *The Principles of Private Detection* that the way to get people to see things from your point of view was to share their anxieties. *Find out what they're worried about*, he wrote, *and then talk about that*. The one thing that could be guaranteed to trigger concern on Mma Potokwani's part was the welfare of children.

"Oh, there are all sorts of children," said Mma Ramotswe. "Old Naledi is full of children, and they like to play on that wasteland. When word gets out among the children that there is a baby elephant there, they will be onto it like . . . like . . ." She struggled to find the right metaphor, and was about to make some reference to bees and honey when Mma Makutsi interjected: "Like flies on cattle," she said.

"Yes, like that," said Mma Ramotswe. "And what worries me is the thought that these children will be hurt. Even a baby elephant weighs rather a lot, Mma Potokwani. A baby elephant can crush a child very easily — even without meaning to."

Mma Potokwani's frown deepened. "That is very worrying, Mma," she said.

"Yes," said Mma Ramotswe.

"You need to go to the police," said Mma Potokwani. "Or the Wildlife Department."

Mma Ramotswe shook her head. "I wish it were that simple, Mma Potokwani. Fanwell suggested that to Charlie. He said, 'Why don't you go to the Wildlife

Department, Charlie, and get them to take this elephant from you?' "

"And?" asked Mma Potokwani.

"Charlie told Fanwell that his friend was unwilling to do that for some reason. Perhaps he thinks he'll get into trouble for moving an elephant without their permission."

"And the police?" asked Mma Potokwani.

"Charlie's friend said the police would just dump it somewhere. They are too busy with all the work they have to do. They can't look after elephants."

Mma Potokwani poured more tea. "This is not very good," she said. "We can't let it hurt the children in Old Naledi." She paused. "Is there something else, Mma Makutsi? Is there something you haven't mentioned?"

Mma Makutsi hesitated. "I think they may be planning to slaughter it and sell the meat. Not Charlie, but his friend. He knows a butcher, apparently."

Mma Potokwani put down the teapot rapidly. "That is very bad news indeed, Mma." She sank her head in her hands. "We don't want the poor creature to die. All the time these poor elephants have been dying, dying. They are very intelligent beasts, Mma."

What she said was heartfelt, and it brought about a short silence. Mma Potokwani had spent her life looking after people who could not look after themselves — her orphans — and she had done so with little fuss and certainly with no thought of personal reward. And it was that same sympathy that had sustained her efforts in that direction, that was now

149

aroused for this small elephant. She was practical, of course — she could not have achieved what she had achieved without knowing how the world worked — and she knew that difficult issues arose when elephants came into contact with human society, but that did not stop the prompting of her heart.

"You can see it in their eyes," said Mma Makutsi. "You can see that they are thinking about you when they look at you. They are very wise creatures."

"And they have very good memories," said Mma Ramotswe. "They remember all the sad things that have happened to them. That is why an elephant often looks sad."

"It's a pity there isn't somebody who can help," said Mma Makutsi.

"I think there is," said Mma Potokwani. "I think I know some people."

Mma Ramotswe looked relieved. "I thought you might, Mma."

"But I will have to get in touch with them," cautioned Mma Potokwani. "And in the meantime . . ."

"In the meantime," ventured Mma Ramotswe, "we need to find some kind person who —"

"Who is used to dealing with orphans," interjected Mma Makutsi.

"Yes," said Mma Ramotswe. "Who is used to dealing with orphans and who would be able to find a safe place for this elephant until something is arranged. That would not be too long, I think."

"No more than a few weeks, I imagine," said Mma Makutsi.

There was silence. From outside, there drifted into Mma Potokwani's office the sound of children chanting a counting rhyme. Mma Ramotswe caught the words, and raised a finger. "I remember that," she said. "I remember that from a long time ago." It was a sound from the old Botswana — the Botswana of her childhood, when everything was quieter and more certain; when people had time for one another. It made her sad to think about that — how people had stopped having time for each other. Well, they hadn't altogether, but it did seem that we all had less time for others in our lives. People had more material things than they used to: they had more money; they had cars; they had more food than they could eat; they had fridges purring away in their kitchens, but what had they lost? What silences, rich and peaceful, had been pushed out of the way by humming machinery?

Mma Potokwani was staring at the ceiling. "It's always possible that we could —" She broke off.

Mma Ramotswe pressed her. "Could what, Mma?"

"That we could use the old cattle stockade we have. It's down at the other end of the vegetable garden — on the edge of the bush there. It is still strong — they used tree trunks to make it."

Mma Ramotswe pretended to be surprised. "I wasn't thinking of you, Mma, but —"

Mma Potokwani cut her short. Her tone was reproving, but, at the same time, fond. "Yes you were, Mma Ramotswe. And you too, Mma Makutsi. You were both thinking of me, but I don't mind, Bomma, because I would have been disappointed if you did *not* think of me. Because I'm *the* orphan lady, am I not? And if I won't help, then who will?"

Neither of her guests spoke. There was only one answer, of course.

"This will only be temporary," continued Mma Potokwani. "I will have to get in touch with my friend to see if she can provide a permanent home. Young people — and young elephants are probably no different — need a proper place. They need somewhere they can stay for a long time."

"I think you put it very well, Mma," said Mma Ramotswe. "You put it perfectly, in fact."

"Thank you, Mma," said Mma Potokwani, reaching for the cake tin. "And since we are all agreed on that, perhaps we should agree on a final slice of cake."

"There will be no argument about that," said Mma Ramotswe. And she was about to say "Even from Mma Makutsi . . ." but did not, of course, because Mma Ramotswe knew when not to say that which she was about to say — a rare gift, not shared by everybody.

The cake was completely finished, only a few crumbs remaining in the bottom of the tin. But that was no surprise because the adage "You cannot have your cake and eat it" was one of those sayings that was incontestably true, as Mma Ramotswe, and indeed Mma Makutsi, and Mma Potokwani too, had discovered on many an occasion.

CHAPTER
NINE

Mma Ramotswe Has Few Faults

They returned to the office, where Mma Ramotswe called what she termed an "extraordinary general meeting". This was a rare occurrence, justified only in the most pressing or extreme circumstances, and involving the attendance of everybody present in the office and the garage. On this occasion, that meant Mma Ramotswe and Mma Makutsi, Fanwell and Mr J. L. B. Matekoni, the last two participants being dragged away somewhat reluctantly from a particularly interesting gearbox issue in an old Ford.

Mr J. L. B. Matekoni was not one to grumble, but he did so now — in his very mild way — pointing out to Mma Ramotswe that you did not normally call a surgeon out from theatre when he was engaged in a delicate surgical procedure. "It's the same with gearboxes," he said. "If you take them to pieces and then walk away you can end up in a terrible mess."

"The boss is right," said Fanwell, nodding sagely. "A terrible mess."

Mma Ramotswe explained that a co-ordinated plan of action needed to be decided then and there.

"We can't let this matter ride," she said. "That young elephant could cause serious harm. Children are likely to find out about his presence, and you know what they are like. Somebody could get hurt."

They sat in the office while Mma Ramotswe told the two mechanics about their conversation with Mma Potokwani. "She was very helpful," she said. "We did not have to spend a long time persuading her."

"We did not have to spend any time at all," said Mma Makutsi. "She made her offer very quickly."

"They have an old cattle stockade," said Mma Ramotswe. "They haven't used it for years . . ."

Mr J. L. B. Matekoni nodded his head. "Yes, I know where that is. At the end of the vegetable gardens. They used it in the old days when the orphan farm had a small herd. The children loved having the cattle but they stopped keeping them when one of them was hit by a truck. The children were so upset by this that Mma Potokwani — or her predecessor, perhaps — said that it was better not to have cattle if that sort of thing was going to happen."

"It's good for children to be brought up with cattle," said Mma Makutsi. "Then they understand. Phuti says that he had his first cattle when he was three."

Mma Ramotswe frowned. "That's a bit young, surely. You cannot look after cattle when you're that young."

Mma Makutsi pursed her lips. "Phuti was very advanced, Mma. He has always been advanced."

Mma Ramotswe did not argue. Mma Makutsi was fiercely loyal to her husband. "The point is," she continued, "that Mma Potokwani has offered to take this elephant while arrangements are being made to get it back up north. Apparently, there is a place up there that will look after elephants who have lost their mothers. But it might take a little while to arrange. It will be safe at the Orphan Farm, in that old stockade."

"Then that is what Charlie must do," said Mr J. L. B. Matekoni. "We must tell him."

Fanwell looked doubtful. "But Charlie wants to keep it at his uncle's place. He says that it's fine there. He doesn't see a problem."

"But there *is* a problem," said Mma Makutsi. "That elephant is going to hurt somebody. It's all very well for Charlie to say that it's all quite safe, but it isn't really. What happens when Charlie comes to work? He says everything is looked after by that young cousin of his, the one who wets the bed . . ."

Fanwell objected. "But that is not his fault, Mma Makutsi. He can't help wetting the bed — and anyway it's nothing to do with what we're talking about."

Mma Makutsi was dismissive. "If a boy wets the bed when he's as old as that boy, then there's an issue, Fanwell. And that issue is what we call psychological. You can't have boys with psychological issues looking after elephants."

Fanwell looked outraged. He turned to Mr J. L. B. Matekoni. This was typical, he thought, of the general attack on men. That boy might be a bed-wetter but there were plenty of girls who wet the bed — weren't there? — anyway, the point was that the competence of boys in general should not be called into question over such an irrelevant matter. Now he said to Mr J. L. B. Matekoni, "She can't say that, Rra, can she? She can't say that that boy can't do something like look after an elephant just because he wets the bed?"

Mr J. L. B. Matekoni, who was sitting in the client's chair next to Mma Ramotswe's desk, shifted his feet uncomfortably. "I don't think a medical problem should affect your ability to do something like look after livestock. No, I don't think that — on balance."

"Livestock?" said Mma Makutsi, her voice raised. "Is an elephant *livestock*, Rra? An elephant is a wild creature — it is not livestock. A lion is not livestock. A giraffe is not livestock."

"What about an ostrich?" Fanwell challenged. "What about ostriches then? You answer me that, Mma Makutsi. Look at those ostrich farms — they'd say that their ostriches are livestock, I'd say. And yet, what is the difference between an ostrich and a lion?"

Mma Makutsi snorted. "If you can't tell that, Fanwell, you'd better keep out of the bush. It would be very bad for you if you were walking through the bush one day and you saw a lion and you thought: oh, that lion will just fly away. That would not be very good, I'd say."

Mr J. L. B. Matekoni intervened. "Ostriches cannot fly, Mma. They have wings, but you never see them fly. They are too large."

Mma Makutsi turned to him. "What are their wings for, then, Rra? You tell me that. If ostriches cannot fly, then why do they have wings?"

Mma Ramotswe sighed. This was an extraordinary general meeting, and here they were immersed in a pointless argument about the capabilities of ostriches. Of course ostriches could not fly — you saw them running through the bush on those long legs of theirs, but you never saw them fly. But the question as to why ostriches had wings was an interesting one, she reflected, even if it was not one that they should be considering at that particular time.

"Not everything in nature has a purpose," said Fanwell.

"Fanwell," said Mma Ramotswe, "we do not need to talk about that."

Fanwell looked indignant. "I didn't start it, Mma. It was Mma Makutsi who started talking about ostriches and lions and so on. All I'm saying is that there are things that have happened because of evolution." He cast a glance in Mma Makutsi's direction. "That is very important, you see — evolution." He paused. "Have you heard of that, Mma Makutsi? Have you heard of Einstein and his theory of evolution."

"Don't think I don't know about evolution," said Mma Makutsi. "And, anyway, it wasn't Einstein. He was the person who . . ." She hesitated, but only briefly, not wanting to confuse Einstein with Clovis Andersen. "He was the person was said *E equals mc squared.*"

Fanwell stared at her defiantly. "So? So, what does that mean, Mma. It's all very well to say that sort of thing, Mma, but what does it mean?"

Mma Makutsi waved a hand in the air. "There isn't time to go into that right now, Fanwell. Some other time, I think."

Mr J. L. B. Matekoni thought of something. "I read somewhere that we came from fish. Have you heard that, Mma Ramotswe? Have you heard that we were all fish once?"

Fanwell shook his head in disbelief. "I cannot believe that, Rra. If we were all fish, then how did we get out of the water? How would we have been able to breathe?"

"Perhaps we took a deep breath underwater first," said Mr J. L. B. Matekoni. "Then we got out of the water for a bit, holding our breath for as long as we could. Then we went back into the water again. Gradually we would have spent more time out than in, and that is when we would have started to evolve into monkeys."

Mma Ramotswe had had enough. Clapping her hands, she announced that the topic of evolution, along with the topic of ostriches and lions, was now closed and they should return to the issue of elephants.

"Are you saying," she asked Fanwell, "that Charlie will not want to have the elephant moved to Mma Potokwani's place? Is that what you're saying?"

Fanwell said that he feared that was the case. "You know how Charlie can be, Mma. He is a very stubborn person."

Mma Ramotswe said that she was very sorry to hear that. "I know what you mean, though. There have been occasions in the past when Charlie has dug his heels in and has refused to be moved. When he's doing that, you just can't get him to change his views. He is like a Kgale Hill — a great big rock that's going nowhere. There's no shifting him."

"Do you think he likes having the elephant there?" asked Mma Makutsi. "Is that the problem?"

Fanwell said that he thought it was. "I think the idea of having an elephant appeals to Charlie. After all, how many people have elephants? Hardly any."

Mma Makutsi said she thought Charlie might feel that having an elephant gave him status. "He's always been very sensitive about status," she said, adding, "Largely because he has none, I think."

Mma Ramotswe was not going to let that pass. "That's unkind, Mma. Charlie is an employee of the No. 1 Ladies' Detective Agency. He has the status that goes with that." She paused. Sometimes Mma Makutsi had to be reminded of the country's ideals; not every day, but sometimes. "And the status of being a citizen of this country. That is a status. And being a person — that is a status too, in the eyes of God. God likes all of us — even Charlie."

Mma Makutsi looked chastened. "I didn't say that God didn't like Charlie, Mma. I never said that. He probably likes him a bit — who knows? But I can't imagine that God would want to spend too much time with him. A bit, maybe, but not much."

Fanwell chose to issue a warning. "You'd better be careful, Mma Makutsi. If God heard you talking about Charlie like that, he'd be furious. You'd better be careful — unless you've got a very good lightning conductor."

"Come now, everybody," said Mma Ramotswe. "Let us not get bogged down in these things." First it had been ostriches and lions and evolution, and now it was theology. She would have to steer the discussion back to where it should be.

"If Charlie won't agree to move the elephant," she said, "then he could find himself in big trouble. If a child were to be knocked over — crushed, even — then Charlie would almost certainly be arrested. If a life were lost, then it could even be manslaughter, which is a very serious offence in the Botswana Penal Code. It is there, you know, manslaughter, for just this sort of situation."

"And that can mean years in prison," said Mma Makutsi. "We would not want that, would we?"

"I would not want anybody to go to prison," said Mr J. L. B. Matekoni.

"Except those people who deserve it," said Mma Makutsi quickly. "There are some people who should definitely be in prison."

Mma Ramotswe made another effort to focus the discussion. "Charlie is the problem here," she said. "You know what Clovis Andersen says . . ."

Mma Makutsi looked up. Mma Ramotswe had few faults, she thought, but if there was one respect in which she might perhaps be criticised, it was in her tendency to attribute quotes to people who almost certainly never said anything of the sort. She did that a great deal with Sereste Khama, who, if Mma Ramotswe were to be believed, gave wise rulings on almost every conceivable subject. Some of these were undoubtedly true — Seretse Khama had been a very wise man indeed — but others, Mma Makutsi suspected, were Mma Ramotswe's own opinions falsely, even if quite innocently, attributed to the great man. So, she thought, it was highly unlikely that Seretse Khama had ever said anything about the benefits of redbush tea, even if Mma Ramotswe had on more than one occasion said that Seretse Khama was one of the first public advocates of redbush tea and that he endorsed the view that it was good for the digestion. Similarly, she very much doubted whether Seretse Khama had ever had cause to remark on the need to soak dried beans overnight before cooking them. He *may* have known about that — although it was not the sort of thing that anybody would expect a man to know — but would he have thought it right for him to speak in his role as Paramount Chief of the Bamangwato people and then as President of Botswana, on such a subject? She thought not, and so she maintained a certain scepticism when Mma Ramotswe spoke of these matters. Mma Makutsi did not fully appreciate, of course, that even if Mma Ramotswe was not absolutely certain that Seretse Khama had pronounced on a matter, she restricted herself to attributing a claim to that effect to those instances where she felt that he would almost certainly have expressed such a view had he turned his mind to the matter. That was quite different from making something up — a distinction that Mma Makutsi, for all *her* many merits, was unlikely to appreciate, given her own tendency to see the world in absolute terms. Not that Mma Ramotswe would ever overtly take her to task for that — in a world in which there were far too many people prepared to tolerate the sort of moral ambiguity or obfuscation that was at odds with the old

Botswana sense of what was right or wrong — in such a world it was refreshing to come across somebody like Mma Makutsi, who had no difficulty at all in drawing a clear and robust line between right and wrong. And it was quite proper, too, that such standards should be defended by the No. 1 Ladies' Detective Agency, because if you could not trust a detective agency to be on the right side, then what hope was there for anything? If there was any institution in which people might expect to find a firm expression of rectitude, then surely it was a detective agency whose mission statement was to get to the bottom of things in the pursuit of justice and the truth — or something to that effect, the precise wording having been lost when Mma Makutsi inadvertently threw out the file in which she had lodged the relevant piece of paper recording the statement.

But now Mma Makutsi was waiting for Mma Ramotswe to reveal what it was that Clovis Andersen had said that was relevant here. It came after a short delay: "You know what Clovis Andersen says — he says find the person who has the solution and then you will find the solution."

Mma Makutsi looked at Mma Ramotswe. "Did he say that, Mma? Are you sure?"

Any further discussion of the source of this proposition was cut short by Mr J. L. B. Matekoni's intervention. "That is very true, Mma," he said. "And in this case, it means that there is only one way of preventing a disaster — and that is to take Charlie out of the picture."

This remark brought a gasp of astonishment from Fanwell. "Take Charlie out?" he stuttered. "Do you mean *kill him*, boss?"

Mr J. L. B. Matekoni rolled his eyes. "Kill Charlie? Don't be ridiculous, Fanwell. You mustn't talk like that."

"But I wasn't talking like that," protested Fanwell. "You were, boss. You said —"

Mma Ramotswe raised a hand to silence the debate. "I think there's a misunderstanding here. I think that what Mr J. L. B. Matekoni meant was that Charlie's views have to be overridden. That is definitely not the same thing as killing him." She looked nervously at Mr J. L. B. Matekoni. "I am right, aren't I, Rra . . . I hope."

Mr J. L. B. Matekoni nodded. "Of course you are, Mma. I'm a mechanic, not a gangster."

Mma Makutsi laughed. "That is very funny," she said. "Fanwell has obviously been watching too many films about gangsters and so on. Those people talk about *taking people out* . . ."

"Rubbing them out," said Fanwell. "That also happens a lot. People rub other people out."

Mma Ramotswe shook her head. "I do not like language like that. We do not speak like that in this country. There can be no rubbing out here."

"No," said Mr J. L. B. Matekoni. "You are right, Mma."

"So, what *do* we do?" asked Fanwell.

Mma Ramotswe looked thoughtful. "I think we have no alternative but to get the elephant away from that place . . ."

Mma Makutsi took over. "And take it to another place — to Mma Potokwani's, in fact. And that means, I think, that we shall have to do it at night." She smiled. "I can just see Charlie's face when he wakes up and finds there is no elephant any longer."

"It would be for the best, I suppose," said Mma Ramotswe. She felt uneasy, and it showed in her expression.

"I don't think we should do it at night," said Fanwell. "The police often patrol Old Naledi at night. You see them driving about in their cars. That is because it's a good place for criminals to walk around at night. They like walking around that place."

Mr J. L. B. Matekoni looked doubtful. "But can we drive through the streets of Gaborone with an elephant in the back of the van? I don't think so. In fact, I don't think we should go behind Charlie's back like this after all. I think it's wrong." He paused, letting his gaze dwell on Mma Makutsi and Mma Ramotswe. "It's just wrong to do something like that."

Fanwell looked uncomfortable. "I think you may be right, boss. Maybe I should have another talk with Charlie. I could try to persuade him."

Mma Ramotswe made up her mind. "Yes," she said. "Speak to him, Fanwell. I'll lend you the van to go round there this evening. Get him to see sense."

The meeting came to an end. Mma Makutsi collected the mugs from which everybody attending the meeting had been drinking. As she washed them at the sink, she addressed Mma Ramotswe over her shoulder.

164

"Why is it, Mma," she asked, "that the best way of putting off a decision is to have a meeting about it?"

Mma Ramotswe laughed. "That is a very interesting question, Mma Makutsi," she said. And then something occurred to her. "And why is it," she continued, "that the best way of not answering a question is to ask it in the first place?"

Mma Makutsi stared at her, adjusting her new glasses at the end of her nose. "Did Clovis Andersen say that, Mma? It's a very interesting thing to say."

Mma Ramotswe shook her head. "No, I said it, Mma Makutsi." She paused. "But it is the sort of thing he says, I think."

They both laughed. Mma Ramotswe watched as Mma Makutsi took off her glasses and polished them with her handkerchief. That was the third time she had done that since the beginning of their extraordinary general meeting. Many people would not remark on that — perhaps not even notice it — but then Mma Ramotswe was a detective, and it was precisely the sort of thing that a detective would notice. And a detective, moreover, might be expected to have a theory as to why people do things more frequently than might normally be expected. *Look for the irregular pattern*, wrote Clovis Andersen . . .

CHAPTER
TEN

They Say She Is Smart, Smart

The following morning Fanwell was waiting for Mma Ramotswe when she arrived at the office. She had travelled into work with Mr J. L. B. Matekoni in his recovery truck, having lent her van to Fanwell. This meant that she had been obliged to occupy the truck's less than comfortable passenger seat and to tolerate, too, a window that rattled loudly, a floor that vibrated beneath her feet, and that curious smell of fuel and grease that was such a recognisable feature of her husband's working space. Her van might not have been the most sophisticated of vehicles — indeed, it was a vehicle of no sophistication at all — but it had her things in it: her work-in-progress teapot cover, a crochet project to keep boredom at bay when she was parked somewhere in the course of an investigation; the small jar of salted peanuts that she kept topped up for dietary emergencies; and the spare pair of dark glasses that served both as protection for the eyes on a particularly sunny day and as an aid — of dubious efficacy, but still — for circumstances in which she felt the need to disguise herself. And, of course, the cab of her van had its own smell, the source of which she had

166

never been able to trace, but that seemed, curiously, to be redolent of freshly baked bread — that enticing smell that drifted out of a bakery when they were taking a batch of loaves out of the oven. It was one of her favourite smells, but she had been unable to work out how it occurred in her van. Had a loaf of bread slipped out of her shopping bag and disappeared down the back of the seat? The back of any seat was a rich source of unexpected and delightful finds — frequently money — but it might also conceal a long-lost brooch, a watch, a pen that still had enough ink in it to write, or occasionally a wrapped and still edible tube of peppermints or some such treat. But a search had revealed no bread, and the smell remained a mystery — overtaken recently by the mystery, now solved, of the elephant smell.

There was the van waiting for her, parked where she always parked it herself, under the acacia tree at the back of the building that housed both Tlokweng Road Speedy Motors and the office of the No. 1 Ladies' Detective Agency. And there were both Fanwell and Charlie standing beside it, Charlie wearing earphones and listening to the radio station that he would listen to constantly if given the chance. It was a particularly noisy station whose tinny outpourings could be heard escaping from the earphones like the chirrup of some tireless electronic cicada somewhere.

Charlie took off his earphones as they approached.

"No problem, Mma Ramotswe," he said. "All agreed. No problem, ya!"

Fanwell explained. "Charlie says that the elephant can go to Mma Potokwani. He has spoken to his friend, and his friend says that is fine with him."

Charlie grinned broadly. "He's pleased that you've found that place up north to take him," he said. "He says to thank you very much for solving the problem. And me too — I was running out of milk formula stuff. That little creature drinks and drinks. Milk, more milk . . . Ow!"

"We haven't arranged a place yet," Mma Ramotswe pointed out. "We are going to try. But there will be formalities."

Charlie sighed in an exaggerated way. "Formalities, Mma, formalities. There are too many formalities in this country. Soon there will be formalities before you're allowed to breathe."

Mma Ramotswe took the keys of the van from Fanwell as she answered Charlie. "Things have to be done a certain way, Charlie. That is just one of these things."

"A pity," said Charlie.

It was one of those days when Charlie's time was allocated to the garage rather than the agency, and so Mma Ramotswe spent the next twenty minutes alone in the office before Mma Makutsi arrived for work. Then the kettle was switched on and the first cup of tea of the day was prepared and served — if one did not count the two cups consumed at home before leaving for work. The excitement caused by the elephant had rather overshadowed other demands on Mma Ramotswe's attention, and now it was time to deal with those. That meant the awkward issue of Blessing and her request for help — an issue that Mma Ramotswe wanted to get out of the way. It would have been simple enough to turn Blessing down and leave it at that, but Mma Ramotswe felt uncomfortable about acting in a way that was contrary to the Botswana tradition of helping a relative if it was remotely within one's power to do so. Even Mma Makutsi, who had reached her own view on this case — and decided that Tefo was a fraud and Blessing was one of those people taken advantage of by a stronger, manipulative man — would acknowledge that a request of this nature had to be given due weight and looked into before being robustly rejected.

Mma Ramotswe had, in fact, decided to ask Mma Makutsi to carry out the next stage of the investigation as she had a quite separate matter, a delicate issue of matrimonial property, with which she was required to deal. This involved a divorce in which the wife was convinced that the husband was concealing assets from the court so as to minimise the divorce settlement. It was an old and familiar issue: men were always trying to hide their business assets; in this case the husband was thought to be hiding an expensive Mercedes-Benz, a substantial number of cattle, and, of all things, a house. The Mercedes-Benz was believed to be parked at his girlfriend's place — but when Mma Ramotswe had gone there it was nowhere to be seen. There were, however, tyre tracks that, when measured, were the exact width of the wheelbase of the model of car he was alleged to be hiding. The cattle proved to be more difficult to track down, but Mma Ramotswe had managed to find a livestock agent who had handled some of them and arranged a transfer from one cattle post to another. The herdsman who had been in charge of that move had been underpaid by the owner and was only too happy to confirm ownership of the cattle. So that left only the house to be located, and she had a plan for that. She would phone the husband and offer to sell him property insurance at a markedly reduced rate. If he rose to the bait and took up her offer of a free insurance survey, then she might expect to be given the address of the missing property. It was a standard trick of the trade, but she believed that it might work. A man who was prepared to hide property on that scale in order to defeat the legitimate claim of a wife of fifteen years who was still looking after three of his young children, might also be expected to be a man who would be interested in the prospect of saving money on insurance. But first she had to find his telephone number: he had recently changed it and had refused to notify his wife of the new number. That was her task that morning — to track down his known associates and see whether she might get the number from them.

She explained to Mma Makutsi what was required. "I know you don't trust that man, Tefo," she began.

"I certainly don't, Mma. I don't trust him even that much." Mma Makutsi indicated a sliver of distance between her thumb and forefinger.

"Not even that, Mma."

"You may be right," said Mma Ramotswe. "But I'd feel more comfortable having some evidence."

Mma Makutsi took a more robust view of the need for evidence when something was as obvious as she thought Tefo's dishonesty was. "If you're pretending your leg's sore, you should at least remember which leg it is," she said dismissively.

"Possibly," said Mma Ramotswe.

"No, Mma, not possibly — definitely. I *know* that man's lying. I knew it straight away. And that Blessing, too. She's a number one big liar, Mma."

"Even so, Mma Makutsi, I'd like you to check on his story." Mma Ramotswe paused, and looked at her colleague. Mma Makutsi had come a long way since those early days when she had joined the agency as a secretary, but she still had her impetuosity to conquer. "Now, Mma, do you remember my old friend, Mma Phiri? Remember her? She was a magistrate, but then she became ill and they gave her early retirement. She was only forty-eight, but the government was very good to her. She lost a lung. One whole lung, Mma."

Mma Makutsi frowned. There had been a Phiri at the college — a very quiet girl who was a prominent Seventh-Day Adventist. She recalled she had refused to drink tea for some reason, but she did not remember much else about her. It was a common enough name, but it was possible they were the same family, even if she did not remember a Phiri who was a magistrate.

"She came to see me once in the office — after she had retired," Mma Ramotswe continued. "Perhaps you were out at the time."

Mma Makutsi waited.

171

"She retired out near Tlokweng," said Mma Ramotswe. "Not far from Mma Potokwani, as it happens. I think she sees her from time to time. You know how she ropes people in to do things for the Orphan Farm. She used to get her to help her with the books — she has a very good memory, Mma. She remembers everything."

"She is very lucky," said Mma Makutsi. "If you remember everything, then you'll forget nothing."

Mma Ramotswe thought about this. It was undoubtedly true, although she was not sure that it really needed to be said. "I'd like you to go and see her," she said. "See if she knows anything about Tefo. We've been told that he was convicted of stock theft. If that's true, then she will know something about it. She knew exactly what everybody was up to. She saw them in court if they did anything illegal. She knew everything — she still does, I think."

Mma Makutsi nodded. "I'll ask her about that man. We'll see what she says. Mind you, I don't really need any confirmation of what I already know, Mma Ramotswe."

Mma Ramotswe thought about what Clovis Andersen said about keeping an open mind, but she could not remember his precise words and she decided that this was not the time to extemporise.

Mma Makutsi drove slowly down the dirt road that ran past the clinic at Tlokweng. The clinic was the reference point, Mma Ramotswe had told her: the third turning after the clinic, she had said, was the Phiri turning. The

172

former magistrate's house was one of several at the end of a track, the others being occupied by the families of her two brothers, both of whom were successful cattle traders.

She slowed down as she drove past the clinic, noticing the handful of people seated on the waiting benches. They were lined up outside, shielded from the sun by an expanse of thick shade netting strung across supporting wooden posts; five of them, including a woman with a baby wrapped in a folded shawl across her back. Mma Makutsi stared at the woman from her car, and for a moment their eyes met, across yards of dusty foreground; and Mma Makutsi thought: my sister, my sister . . . She had no idea who the woman was, but she felt a sudden surge of feeling for her — a feeling of sympathy so intense that it surprised her. She was just a stranger — a woman whom she had never seen before and would never see again. All she had to do was to continue with her journey, to turn the corner ahead, and it would be as if the other woman had ceased to exist. That was what you could do with most people you encountered in this life: you just continued to do what you were already doing and you passed them by, because you simply could not stop at every moment and think: this is the only time I'm going to see this person on this earth and . . . You could not do that because you did not have enough time. There was not enough time, and you were only one person, one small person — because every person, even the largest of us, is still just a small thing when you come to think of it — and there is only so much that one person can do about anything. So there she was, Mma Makutsi, who could have been where that other woman was, and instead was there in her car, with a fine house to return to, and a husband with cattle — and a furniture store — and a job that made her someone when previously she had been nobody in particular; and it had all started in Bobonong and there were plenty of people who were still stuck back there and would never be able to leave; never be able to go off to the Botswana Secretarial College and end up with ninety-seven per cent. For most of the world got nowhere near ninety-seven per cent in their examinations, they simply did not, and . . . That poor woman with her child — whatever number of children it was — whose life would be a constant battle, as likely as not. A battle against poverty, a battle to get enough food for her other children, a battle to wash the children's clothes and keep the baby clean, and . . .

She stopped her car. She was level with the clinic gate, and by reversing a few yards she was able to turn directly into the short drive that led up to the clinic. She parked the car next to another car that was already there — the doctor's or the nurse's, perhaps — and then she got out and walked up to the waiting patients. They watched her carefully — as if judging her. They would have seen the car, she realised — a new model, belonging to Phuti — and they would have made up their minds about her. These were not well-off people, and they would have decided that there was a wide gulf between them and her.

174

She greeted them in the old-fashioned way, and they responded politely. She sat down on the bench, next to the woman with the baby.

"I saw you from the car, my sister. I saw you waiting here."

The woman looked at her over the baby's head. She did not at first respond to Mma Makutsi's remark, but seemed to be waiting for something else.

"So, you are waiting for the doctor?" said Mma Makutsi.

The woman shook her head. "There is a nurse — that is all." She spoke quietly, as if she were uncomfortable about disturbing the quiet that lay about them; for the others were silent, and were listening as they watched. And all that there was, all that could be heard about them, was the sound of the cicadas screeching away, as they liked to do in the heat, determined that their hidden kind, concealed in the private places of insects, should hear them and take notice.

Mma Makutsi persisted. "For the baby? You're taking the baby to the nurse? Or is it for yourself?"

The woman sighed — a sigh that came from a hinterland of acceptance: this is the way the world is. This is what it is like. "It is for the baby," she said. "She is crying, crying, crying after I feed her. She never stops — except when I come here. Then she is silent."

Mma Makutsi clicked her tongue almost inaudibly — the sound, in Botswana, of a sympathy that may be felt, even if it is hard to put into words. But then she said, "It is always like that. Children do not do what

you want them to do, do they? They do the opposite."
She looked at the baby, at its tiny head in its heavy wool
cap — even in this heat, which surely would make the
child's head too hot. A lighter, breathable cloth, white
muslin and at least cooler-looking, covered the child's
face, so that only the eyes and forehead were showing.
"That sounds like *kgadikêgo*, Mma. That is what babies
get sometimes — and it makes them cry a lot." She
used the Setswana word, *kgadikêgo* — stomach ache.

The woman patted her baby through the cloth of the
sling. "You're right, Mma," she said. "They call it colic
these days. It is probably that. Of course, the children
themselves don't understand."

"No, they don't." Mma Makutsi reached out to
touch the baby lightly, against the cheek. The child's
small eyes watched her.

"You want to see the nurse too?" asked the woman.
"She is very good at her job, this nurse."

Mma Makutsi shook her head. "No, I do not need to
see the nurse. I was just driving past and I saw you and
your baby and thought . . ." She stopped. What had she
thought? She was not sure; it was difficult to give
sympathy a specific shape. And then it came to her: "I
wondered whether you lived close by, or whether you
had to walk here."

The woman pointed. "I live that way, Mma. About
four miles — maybe five. I had to walk here."

"That is not easy," said Mma Makutsi. "It is not easy
in the heat — especially if you're carrying a baby."

"I am used to it," said the woman. "If you're used to
something, then it is not so hard."

Mma Makutsi looked over her shoulder at her car. "That car has lots of room, Mma. There will be room for you and your baby. I can take you home after you've seen the nurse."

The woman stared at her in apparent disbelief. "But Mma, but . . ."

Mma Makutsi touched her lightly on the forearm to stem her protestations. "My mind is made up, Mma."

The sunlight caught her glasses, and they flashed a warning that she was determined and would not welcome an attempt at dissuasion. Surprised, but nonetheless understanding this, the woman lowered her head and said, "You are very kind, Mma."

Mma Makutsi seated herself on the bench next to the woman. The other people waiting had listened to every word of her conversation with the woman, and one of them, an elderly man, now said, "That lady can go in first, when the nurse is ready. Then she will not hold you up too much, Mma."

Another nodded, and said, "It is very hot."

A third said, "Yes, it is always hot. Always."

A few minutes later, the nurse arrived, parking her car next to Mma Makutsi's. She nodded at the waiting patients before unlocking the clinic. Mma Makutsi sat and stared at the sky while the woman went inside; she heard the baby crying, but only briefly, and then the woman re-emerged, clutching a paper bag on which a label had been stuck.

Mma Makutsi rose to her feet. "Everything is all right, Mma?"

The woman smiled. "She has given me something to give to the baby. She says it will settle the stomach."

They walked to Mma Makutsi's car. In the brief period during which it had been parked in the sunlight, the heat within it had built up, even with the windows left open. Mma Makutsi took a newspaper from the passenger seat, unfolded it and spread it over the back seat to protect the woman from the hot upholstery. Then she drove back to the road and followed the woman's directions to her house. In the driver's mirror, she saw the baby resting on her mother's lap. She saw a tiny hand reach out and grasp the woman's fingers. She remembered how her own baby, Itumelang Andersen Radiphuti, had done this when he had first been introduced to his father, and how Phuti had wept with emotion and said, "He's shaking hands with his daddy — see, that's what he is doing — he's shaking hands." And she had fought back the tears, too, because only a few years earlier she would never have dreamed that she would have this in her life: a kind husband who loved her — and often told her so — and a healthy baby. And a house. And cattle. And a vegetable garden. And enough dresses to wear a different one every day for three weeks if she wanted to. How had all that happened?

It did not take long to reach the woman's house. Years earlier, when Mma Makutsi had still been in Bobonong, a house of this size and simplicity would not have been unusual — a single room, effectively, with a sloping roof of corrugated tin and walls of distempered daub. Now, with the prosperity that the country had

178

enjoyed, the steady economic progress that the diamond mines, cautious husbandry, and good government had brought to the country, the ranks of those still living in single-room houses — huts, really — had been steadily thinned. People now had at least two or three rooms; they had walls made of breeze blocks; they had running water or at least access to a stand-pipe supplied by a village borehole. And yet there were still those whom this amelioration had bypassed, and who could not afford more than the most cramped living quarters. As the woman in the back seat reached forward to tap her on the shoulder, Mma Makutsi realised that this woman was one of those who had not been invited within the fold of plenty. It was no surprise, really, as she had expected something of this sort, but she found herself drawing in her breath as she took in the meanness of her new friend's home.

"This is my place here, Mma. This is it."

Mma Makutsi nosed the car over the last few bumps of eroded track. "To your doorstep, Mma," she said, trying to sound as cheery as she could.

She stopped the car.

"I would like to make you some tea, Mma," said the woman. "There is no milk, but there is some tea."

Mma Makutsi looked at her watch. "I would like to say yes, Mma," she said. "I would like that very much, but I have to go and see somebody and she will be sitting there thinking: where is this woman who was coming to see me? She will be thinking: this woman is a very rude woman who is always late."

They both laughed.

"Maybe some other time, Mma," said the woman.

Mma Makutsi got out of her car to help the woman. She said, "May I hold your baby? Just for a minute or two?"

"Of course, Mma," said the woman. "Here she is."

She handed the infant to Mma Makutsi, who took her gently, a precious, fragile parcel of humanity. And as she did so, the muslin cloth that had obscured the child's face fell away, and Mma Makutsi saw the cleft lip. Her gaze dwelt on it for a few seconds, and then passed to the woman. She had not intended that her shock should show, but it did; she could not conceal it.

"She is going to have an operation," said the woman. "They are going to do it down in Gaborone, at the big hospital there."

"I see, Mma. That is good. They can fix these things now, can't they?"

The woman inclined her head. "Yes." Then she added, "My sister will take her there."

Mma Makutsi stroked the baby's cheek. "She is very beautiful, Mma. Look at her eyes. They are lovely eyes."

A smile crossed the woman's face. "They are like the eyes of my late mother."

"Eyes run in families," said Mma Makutsi. "That often happens." She paused. "Your sister, Mma? What about you? Wouldn't it be better for you to go with her?"

The woman did not answer.

"How long will she be there?" Mma Makutsi pressed.

180

"Five days," said the woman. "They said five days. My sister is in Gaborone. She works in one of the big hotels, but she will be able to visit her every other day."

Mma Makutsi drew in her breath. "But it will be hard for a little baby not to have her mother there, Mma."

The woman sighed. "I cannot go, Mma. I am working at that school over there." She pointed towards the village centre. "I am one of the cooks. The man who is in charge is very strict. He says that I can go, but I will not be paid for a whole week. And if that happens, then I cannot buy food for my mother, and my brother, too — he is one of those people who cannot work because something went wrong when he was being born and it is very hard for him to walk, Mma."

Mma Makutsi held the child close to her. She felt its breath against her cheek — a tiny movement of air, like the touch of a feather. There was only one thing for her to do — and she did it.

"I can help you, Mma. I can help you to go to Gaborone."

"That is kind of you, Mma. But that is not why I cannot go. There are minibuses, but I cannot go because —"

Mma Makutsi handed the baby back. As she did so, she said, "That's not what I meant, Mma. What I meant is that I will give you the money — the same as your wages for that week. I will give it to you. And you can stay at our place if there is no place for you to stay at the hospital."

The woman stared at her. "They have a place for mothers to sleep. You can sleep beside your baby."

"Then that is what you must do," said Mma Makutsi.

The woman held the baby with one arm; with the other she reached and gripped Mma Makutsi's blouse. "Mma, you are the kindest person in this country. That is true, Mma — that is true. You are the kindest person."

Mma Makutsi turned away, embarrassed by the praise. "No, Mma," she said. "You must not call me that. I am the same as everybody else. No different."

"But who would help some person they have just met, Mma? That is why I'm saying what I've just said."

Mma Makutsi became business-like. "I'm going to write down my telephone number, Mma. And then I shall write down our address too. This is where I work, you see." She took a piece of paper from her bag and wrote down the details.

The woman said, "I haven't told you my name, Mma. I am Mma Moyana."

She took the paper and read what Mma Makutsi had written. She looked up in astonishment.

"You are that detective lady? I have seen the sign often when I have gone into town. It's that place just off the Tlokweng Road, isn't it? Next to that garage? The No. 1 Ladies' Detective Agency? You're that lady they talk about?"

Mma Makutsi hesitated. "One of them," she said. "There is another lady there." She hesitated. She had to be honest. "That other lady is called Mma Ramotswe.

She is the one who started the business. I am her . . . her associate."

The woman frowned. "But I have heard there is another one there, who is a very clever detective. They say she is smart, smart, Mma."

Mma Makutsi held her breath. Had word got out about her ninety-seven per cent?

"She is called Mma Makutsi," said the woman. "That is what I have heard."

For a few moments Mma Makutsi did not say anything. But the words that the woman had just uttered hung in the air for all to see, like great letters of smoke written across the sky. She savoured the moment, and then said, struggling to keep her voice even, "Mma, you are the kind one now. Thank you for what you have said. It has made me very happy."

CHAPTER
ELEVEN

My Cup Has Too Much Tea in It

"You will find her a very polite lady," Mma Ramotswe had said of her friend, the retired Mma Phiri. "Many people are polite, Mma — still — but there are some who are very polite. This lady is very polite."

Mma Makutsi nodded. She had met some of these very polite people — most of them ladies, she had to admit, although now that she thought of it there were many very polite men too. Her own husband, Phuti, was one who had a natural courtesy about him that was frequently remarked upon by others, and even her baby, Itumelang Andersen Radiphuti, showed every sign of being a very polite baby. There were many babies who grabbed at anything you offered them — snatched it, in fact — but Itumelang never did that. If you offered him his bottle of milk he would look at you first, as if to secure your permission, as if to say, "Are you sure?" and then he would take it, in both hands, as was the polite thing to do in Botswana. You should never snatch something with a single hand, that was a lesson that parents taught their children at a very early age; but it had not been necessary, it seemed, to give Itumelang that lesson. Presumably that was because manners, although they needed to be taught, could, to a certain extent, be inherited — just as you could inherit a nose or a way of holding your head, or a preference for this food over that food. Mma Makutsi was a strong believer in the inheritance principle: nothing came from nowhere, and most of our ordinary human characteristics were handed down to us from our parents and grandparents, and indeed from the ancestors themselves — those remote, shadowy figures who lived in Botswana so long ago and whose fingerprints, faint and unobtrusive, could be seen upon the land if one cared to look for them.

Of course, inheritance brought bad things as well as good. Violet Sephotho, for instance, was the way she was because earlier Sephothos had been the same, had been interested only in attracting the attentions of men. Mma Makutsi smiled to herself as she imagined Violet's grandmother behaving exactly like her granddaughter, a figure bent with age but still flirting with ancient men, too old to even notice what was going on in the world about them, and certainly immune to the antics of flashy elderly women . . .

But even as these delicious thoughts came to her, she found herself at the front gate of the Phiri household and calling out to those within. She could think about the Sephotho clan later on, when she could perhaps imagine what the next generation would be like — worse than Violet, presumably, because they said that in general inherited qualities got worse as the generations went by. That was especially so if there was inbreeding — if one Sephotho married a distant Sephotho cousin,

185

for example — something allowed by the law and by custom but perhaps not the best tactic for the improvement of stock. That was something she could return to later, and perhaps discuss with Mma Ramotswe, although Mma Ramotswe, being as charitable as she was, would be more tolerant of Sephotho failings than she, Mma Makutsi, was inclined to be. Mma Ramotswe, of course, had not been at the Botswana Secretarial College at the same time as Violet, and could therefore be forgiven for not realising the full awfulness of Violet's behaviour. There was a limit to the amount of tolerance one should show, Mma Makutsi thought; if you were excessively tolerant, unacceptable people — like Violet Sephotho — might imagine that they were all right, whereas the message that society should give to such people was an unambiguous "You are not all right!" That was the problem: not enough people were sending out that signal; not enough people were prepared to shake their heads when they looked at other, unacceptable, people. It was hard work, shaking your head like that, but it had to be done — there was no way round it. And it was hard work, too, having to get up and walk out whenever an unacceptable person entered a room, but that, too, had to be done. There should be far more walking out, Mma Makutsi thought, and as she thought that, from down below, she imagined two thin voices voicing in unison their support for that particular proposition: *too right, boss — count us in on that* . . . Shoes, she thought, know what's what. There is no confusion on the part of shoes when it comes to matters of right and wrong . . .

"Mma Makutsi?" said Mma Phiri, as she opened the door. "Precious said that you would be coming, Mma. You are very welcome."

Mma Makutsi followed her hostess inside. She could not help but reflect on the difference between the house she was now entering and the house she had just left — between the world of Mma Phiri and that of Mma Moyana. Mma Phiri's house had a solid feel to it: it was one of those buildings that looked as if it had always been there, as if it emanated from the very ground upon which it stood. There were some houses like that — they seemed to be in the place where they were *meant* to be; whereas there were other houses, constructions with a much flimsier feel to them, that looked as if they had been dropped on the landscape by some great and unseen hand, and sooner or later — probably sooner — the land would shrug them off.

"You have a very fine house, Mma," said Mma Makutsi.

Mma Phiri gestured for her guest to sit down. Even the sofa at which she pointed, an inviting, cream-coloured three-seater, looked as if it had been there forever, and that the house might have been built around it. There were some sofas that were like that — they had the air, and the confidence, of the thing that had been there first, before walls and roof and other human additions had been built around them. Phuti had a term for that quality in furniture — "permanent furniture". That was how he described some of the items that he sold in his Double Comfort Furniture Store, and she had heard him say to prospective purchasers, "This sofa may be slightly more expensive, but it is what I call *permanent*. It is built to last permanently, you see. This is not a *temporary* sofa. This is a sofa on which your great-grandchildren will be sitting, I think."

As she sat down, it occurred to her that she might have seen the sofa before, just as she vaguely recognised a small cabinet at the far end of the room. And then it dawned on her: this furniture had all the qualities of Double Comfort Furniture Store furniture. It had that *feel*.

She felt the fabric under her hands. Yes, it certainly had that. It was an indefinable quality — one that would be too difficult to put into words, but it could be picked up by the eye, and indeed by the other senses.

"Mma Phiri," she ventured, "do you mind my asking: where did you get this very fine sofa?"

Mma Phiri looked at the sofa with an unmistakable fondness. "I like that sofa very much, Mma," she replied. "There are some sofas that one can take or leave — but that sofa is not one of them. That sofa is very important to me, Mma."

Mma Makutsi nodded encouragingly. "I can see that, Mma."

"There is a big furniture store," Mma Phiri continued. "You may know the place. It is near the old bus station. I forget the name of it . . ."

"The Double Comfort Furniture Store," prompted Mma Makutsi.

"That's it. Yes, that's the name of that place. It belongs to that man with the big nose — you may have seen him."

Mma Makutsi caught her breath. She was not sure whether she should keep silent or whether she should say something, just in case Mma Phiri might be thinking of digging herself deeper into a hole. She decided to speak, but before she could say anything, Mma Phiri continued, "Yes, his nose: you should see —"

"That man is my husband, Mma," said Mma Makutsi.

Mma Phiri froze. "Your husband, Mma? It's his shop?"

"Yes," said Mma Makutsi. "That man is my husband, Mma. He's called Phuti Radiphuti and he is the father of my first-born, Itumelang Andersen Radiphuti."

Mma Makutsi spoke with quiet dignity. As she did so, she thought of Phuti's nose; it was certainly not a small nose, but it was by no means one of the largest in the country. There were several noses right there in Gaborone that were unquestionably larger than Phuti's. There was that man whose picture was often to be seen in the *Botswana Daily News*, that man who was chairman of that foodstuffs company and who was always handing out prizes for this, that and the next thing. What about his nose? And, anyway, Phuti could carry off his nose because he was a large-boned man and he was tall enough to have such a large nose. It was different if you were small; in such a case the overall effect would be a bit unbalanced, and one could very easily look like a hornbill, with its overly prominent beak.

Mma Phiri was quick to recover. "I'm sorry, Mma. I didn't mean to criticise your husband's nose. It was more of a compliment than anything else."

Mma Makutsi sucked in her cheeks. "I see, Mma." She sounded icy; she had not intended to, but she did.

"I've always said that a good nose on a man is a very positive thing," Mma Phiri continued. "These men — these modern men — with their small noses don't realise how ineffective it makes them look. Whereas a man with a prominent, distinguished nose — like your husband's — usually has an air of firmness about him." She paused. "And women find such noses very attractive, I may say, Mma. They are drawn to such noses as . . . as moths are drawn to a candle."

Mma Makutsi frowned. "Am I to conclude, Mma, that you — you personally, that is — are drawn to my husband's nose?"

Mma Phiri bit her lip. "No, Mma — not at all. I am certainly not drawn to your husband's nose. I have not given it a second thought."

"And yet you are the one who brought it up, Mma. We were talking about sofas and suddenly the topic of conversation shifted to noses."

Mma Phiri laughed nervously. "It is a handsome nose, Mma. But I'm sure you know that — you married it." She corrected herself quickly. "I mean, you married your husband."

Mma Makutsi waited.

"And anyway, Mma, that shop — yes, that is where we bought this sofa. It was on sale, I think. Ten per cent off, or something like that, although when people say that prices have been reduced I never really believe them."

Mma Makutsi resumed her icy tone. "My husband always means what he says, Mma — in business as well as in private.

"Of course, Mma. Of course." Mma Phiri looked uncomfortable, and Mma Makutsi, realising that this encounter had got off to a bad start, saw that it was up to her to rescue it. After all, she was here, as Mma Ramotswe's representative, to question Mma Phiri, and there was no point at all in antagonising the person from whom you were asking for information.

She made a placatory remark. "I am very glad that you are pleased with this sofa," she said. "My husband is always keen to please his customers. He'll be very happy when I tell him that you're satisfied with the sofa, Mma."

The tension dispelled, they proceeded to easier subjects. Mma Phiri asked after Mma Ramotswe, and Mma Makutsi told her that Mma Ramotswe was in good health, was very busy, and sent her warmest regards to her old friend. Mma Phiri replied that she hoped Mma Makutsi would pass on her own regards, and assure Mma Ramotswe that she and her entire family were in good health — apart from one grandson, who had broken his arm by falling out of a tree, but had learned his lesson and would undoubtedly be more careful in future.

191

"It is a pity that some lessons have to be learned in a painful way," said Mma Makutsi. "But that is the way the world works, I suppose."

This sage observation brought a nod of agreement from Mma Phiri, followed by silence.

"Mma Ramotswe has asked me to find out something," Mma Makutsi said. "We have an issue, Mma."

Mma Phiri raised an enquiring eyebrow. "One of your cases?"

Mma Makutsi shook her head. "No, it's not exactly a case, Mma. It's more of a . . ." She searched for the right term. What was it? A dilemma? That was it. "It's a dilemma, Mma. We are faced with the issue of whether we do one thing or another. It is that sort of issue."

"Many issues are like that," said Mma Phiri. "My entire professional life, in a way, was just that. Do I do this or that? Do I believe this person or that person? Do I decide this way or another way altogether?"

Mma Makutsi had always been in awe of magistrates and judges, whose job, she thought, was surely one of the most difficult jobs imaginable. When she had been younger — even as recently as a few years ago — she'd been able to make up her mind quickly and then stick to her opinions. She felt that she could sum people up more or less on first meeting, and be reasonably sure that she would not change her mind about them. These days she was not so sure; the world, which in the past had been in sharp enough focus, now seemed rather more blurred. Right and wrong were still there, of course — two gardens side by side, with distinctive

192

flora and fauna — but now the boundary between the two domains was perhaps not quite as distinct as it used to be. During her student days at the Botswana Secretarial College, and indeed when she'd first worked for Mma Ramotswe, there had been no doubt in her mind about many of the issues of the day and their possible solution. In those days she had shown no hesitation in disapproving of people whom she did not like, or those she felt were up to no good. Now it was harder to write people off quite so quickly, with any confidence that one's views would remain stable — with the exception of Violet Sephotho, of course, of whom she held precisely the same opinion as she had done on first acquaintance all those years ago.

She felt emboldened to ask Mma Phiri how she dealt with lies. "How do you tell if somebody's telling the truth, Mma?" she said. "If you're sitting there in court on the . . . on the chair . . ."

"We call it the bench," said Mma Phiri. "The judge sits on a bench. That word has always been used — for some reason. I think it is historical. They must have sat on benches in the old days, way back — in England, I suppose. Nowadays it is really a chair, but we still call it a bench."

Mma Makutsi nodded. "Yes, a bench. You're sitting on the bench and you're listening to a witness, perhaps, and the witness starts to talk. Do you think: is this a truthful person? And how do you answer that, Mma? How can you tell?"

Mma Phiri laughed. "That's a very difficult question, Mma. They don't teach you how to do that, you know.

You go to the University of Botswana and you do a law degree and they teach you all about the law of contract and the law of property and so on. You learn lots and lots of cases and you read and read, Mma, but they never teach you how to look at a witness and work out whether he or she is telling the truth."

"No?"

"No, they do not. They teach you what the rules are — about what you can ask a witness and what you cannot ask, but they don't teach you about how to tell the difference between an honest person and a liar."

"Experience, Mma? Is that it?"

Mma Phiri smiled and folded her hands across her lap. "Yes, experience, Mma. You develop that ability through experience. Most judges and magistrates will tell you that. They know that there are some things you cannot learn by reading a book."

Mma Makutsi agreed with that. It was the same with detective work. Nobody had taught her how to be a detective . . . To begin with, she had fumbled her way into the job, learning by her mistakes, gradually building up a *feeling* for the tasks facing a detective. And the same was true with life in general: you learned as you went through it, as you got older — that was the only way to develop judgement, or wisdom, perhaps, because wisdom really was what we needed if we were to get through life without making too much of a disaster of it. And yet wisdom, however much people may speak about it, was a rare quality, and you did not encounter it every day. Mma Ramotswe had it — Mma Makutsi was sure of that, and Mma Potokwani too, because she had seen so much of life looking after the orphans. And then there were some of the elders who had it — the people who had held office in the government of Botswana, some of the chiefs, retired principals of schools . . . yes, there was wisdom about, if you knew where to look for it. And it was there, she thought — right there in the room with her, in the shape of this former magistrate who had dispensed justice over so many years and must have seen the full range of human nature.

A young woman came in with a tea tray. "This is my daughter," said Mma Phiri.

Mma Makutsi and the daughter greeted one another, before the daughter retreated into the kitchen.

"She has three children," said Mma Phiri. "They keep her very busy because they are still young. But I love having them living with me. It is my great privilege, Mma." She reached forward to pour the tea. "What do you and Mma Ramotswe need to know, Mma?"

Mma Makutsi took a sip of the tea that had been poured. "Five Roses," she said. "This is very good tea."

Mma Phiri smiled. "That shows you are a detective, Mma. Nobody else identifies the brand of tea."

"Am I right, Mma?"

They both laughed. "As it happens, you are," Mma Phiri said. "But you were about to tell me, Mma, what it is that you want to find out."

Mma Makutsi began. "It is about a man who says that he needs an operation. *Says*, Mma. That's what he says, but we are not so sure."

Mma Phiri rolled her eyes. "The usual story, Mma? Money?"

"Yes, but . . . But we are not sure. I think he's lying, but Mma Ramotswe . . . Well, you know how kind she is, Mma Phiri."

"She is very kind, Mma. Everybody knows that. She is a kind lady." She paused. "But tell me, Mma Makutsi, do I know this man?"

"You might, Mma. He may have been one of your clients, so to speak. Or you may know about the case — because Mma Ramotswe says that you are a lady with a very good memory."

Mma Phiri chuckled. "It used to be rather good, yes, but you know how it is when you're getting on . . . Well, you probably don't know at your age, but people like me who have had some big birthdays, we're always asking ourselves: where have I put my spectacles? And then you realise they're on your nose, Mma — that sort of thing."

"Or you remember that you don't wear spectacles in the first place," said Mma Makutsi.

There was a short silence. Then Mma Phiri said, "That is very funny, Mma." And a further pause before, "It isn't quite that bad, Mma. Try me."

There was a faint note of reproach in Mma Phiri's voice, and Mma Makutsi tried to sound as respectful as possible as she explained her quest. She had not gone far, though, before Mma Phiri nodded vigorously and raised a hand to stop her.

"I am very familiar with that case, Mma," she said. "It was some time ago. Twelve years, probably; just before I retired. But yes, I was the magistrate. I remember stock theft cases very clearly because they always involve a lot of passion. People get very upset about them, and sometimes you have to warn people in court — the public, that is — not to sit there and murmur during the evidence."

"You remember that man?"

"Yes, as I said, I remember the case very clearly. This man — this Tefo — was a South African Motswana. I felt a bit sorry for him, actually, because those people are very close to us, as you know. They speak our language — we have the same ancestors, way back, but they are citizens of another country and that is what counts these days. So, they don't have all the things that we have."

Mma Makutsi agreed. It was hard. Botswana was a fortunate country, surrounded by neighbours who were not quite so fortunate. That sort of situation could be as difficult for a country as it could be in ordinary life, where neighbours with a car live next to neighbours without one, or neighbours with curtains live next to neighbours with none. Life was stubbornly unequal, whatever efforts the well-meaning made to reduce the contrast between good fortune and want. One day, perhaps, there would be enough for all, and painful differences of that nature would be no more, or be less obvious, but that day, Mma Makutsi thought, was not one that she would ever see.

"Yes," continued Mma Phiri. "That was one of those cases where you sit there . . ."

"On your bench . . ."

197

"Yes, you sit there on the bench and you see some poor person in front of you. And you have a strong suspicion that he did not do what he is accused of doing, and yet all the evidence is there and you can't just throw the case out because you have a feeling somewhere in your stomach that this is the wrong person. Or you are satisfied that he did it, but there are many good reasons why he did what he did and, worst of all, you think: if I had been there, I would have done exactly the same as he did. You sometimes think that, Mma, and yet you know that the law's the law and people can't take matters into their own hands."

Mma Phiri poured more tea into their cups. "I remember, Mma, I had a case once when a man was charged with assaulting another man and he had taken an axe to him, Mma — a big axe used for chopping wood — and chopped one of his fingers off. Yes, actually chopped it off. The police found the finger and there was a photograph of it in court. And the prosecutor said to the witness — the man whose finger had been chopped off — 'Is that your finger, Rra?' And the witness looked at the photograph and said, 'It is not my finger any longer, sir.' I tell you, Mma Makutsi, that was one of those times when I struggled not to laugh, and yet it was a very sad case because the accused had taken the axe to this other man who had kidnapped his teenage daughter and was planning to sell her to some terrible person in the Congo for forced marriage, Mma. Fortunately, the police stopped him in time, before he could take the girl away, but the father came at him with an axe when he found out." She paused. "What father would not have felt like doing something like that, Mma? I could understand, but the problem is that we cannot allow people to take an axe to anybody who does some terrible thing to them. That is what the law is for."

Mma Makutsi asked what happened.

"I had to give him a prison sentence," said Mma Phiri. "But I suspended it. That is the great thing about suspended sentences. You can make it quite clear that you disapprove of what somebody has done; you can make it clear that there must be punishment; but then you can allow mercy to do its work. Mercy, Mma. Mercy is a very great thing. We must always remember mercy."

Mma Makutsi lowered her eyes. This magistrate was not only a wise woman — she was humane as well. And that reminded Mma Makutsi of the fact that she herself was sometimes a little bit unforgiving — just a little bit. She should try harder, perhaps. And then the image of Violet Sephotho came to mind, and her new resolve was immediately tested — to breaking point, in fact.

"But to get back to your stock theft man," said Mma Phiri. "The reason why I felt uncomfortable in that case was because I thought he was not guilty. And yet he had lodged a guilty plea and did not withdraw it when I gave him the chance. I said, 'Are you sure you don't want to change your plea?' And he said that he did not. But I watched him, Mma, as he spoke, and I saw him looking at a lady sitting in the front row of the public benches. She was a relative of his — I happened to know that — and she had come in with him. She is a

199

woman called Blessing, and I had come across her before."

Mma Makutsi listened attentively.

"She had been up before me," said Mma Phiri.

"In court, Mma?"

"Yes. She had been charged with an offence herself. A year or so earlier."

Mma Makutsi's eyes widened. "She had, Mma? The lady?"

"Yes. Stock theft, as it happens, Mma. A very minor case. She stole a goat."

Mma Makutsi was silent as she absorbed the unexpected information. And yet, she asked herself, why should she be surprised? If Tefo had been lying about his operation, then so too was Blessing.

Mma Phiri explained that stealing a goat was a low-value theft, punishable with a fine. And yet, in the eyes of the law, it was technically a stock theft and that meant that if somebody who stole a goat was subsequently convicted of taking a cow, that would make the second offence all that more serious.

Mma Phiri fixed Mma Makutsi with an enquiring look. "You will see where this is going," she said.

Mma Makutsi looked blank. She suspected she was missing something, but she was not sure what it was. She felt a certain embarrassment now: she might be the great detective who could identify Five Roses tea, but what use was that if she then missed something rather more important?

Mma Phiri, being too polite to embarrass her guest, immediately reassured her. "Of course, it's not obvious

200

at all. It's not what anybody would expect, Mma: the real thief was that woman, Blessing. This other man, this Tefo, was her lover, even her husband for all I knew, and she had got him to take the blame. So, he pleaded guilty, and because he did so, it was difficult for me to do anything but convict him. I could have refused to accept his plea, of course, and discharged him, but the Attorney General gets very cross if a magistrate does that sort of thing."

Mma Makutsi nodded. "Yes, Mma, I see, I see."

Mma Phiri continued, "It was very clear to me, from where I was sitting . . ."

"On your bench . . ."

"On *the* bench, yes, that this was one of those situations where a strong woman has a weak man under her control. She was using him, Mma. You see that sort of thing from time to time: the man is a nothing at all, a useless, and the woman is everything."

Mma Makutsi noted the term "a useless". That was a wonderful description, and she would use it herself, she thought. Every so often one came across "a useless", and sometimes it was difficult to find just the right words to describe such a person. Now she had them: two short and pithy words — one very short and very pithy: "a useless".

She thanked Mma Phiri. "You have told me everything I need to know, Mma. I shall go back to Mma Ramotswe and tell her what you have said."

Mma Phiri saw Mma Makutsi out to her car. "You must pass on a message to your husband," she said, as fond farewells were exchanged. "You must tell him that

201

I sit on that sofa every day. I sit there and think how comfortable it is."

"More comfortable than that bench of yours," said Mma Makutsi.

The joke was well received. "Very much so," said Mma Phiri, laughing. "Perhaps they should put sofas like that in the High Court for the judges there. They would be more comfortable sitting on them while they listened to the arguments of the lawyers." She paused. "Mind you, Mma, the risk is that they would go to sleep."

"That would not do," said Mma Makutsi.

"Definitely not."

As she drove back to the main road, Mma Makutsi reflected with some satisfaction on the afternoon's events. She had met two good women: one with a baby, and a difficult life, and one in much more comfortable circumstances and with a life of achievement behind her. She had found out what she needed to find out. She had enlarged her vocabulary with an excellent term to use, sparingly, when other terms seemed inadequate. And now, after calling in briefly at the office, she was going to go home to a loving husband, a house with a cool veranda, and a young child who meant more to her than anything else in the world. There was a saying that expressed how she felt, but she could not quite remember what it was. It was something to do with cups running over. Cups of tea? Was it about tea? "My cup has too much tea in it"? No, that was not right, but perhaps it expressed, accurately enough, how she felt.

CHAPTER TWELVE

She's a Useless

Everything had been arranged with Mma Potokwani.

"We shall arrive at about half-past eight," Mr J. L. B. Matekoni told her on the telephone. "It will just be me, Charlie and Fanwell."

"And an elephant," added Mma Potokwani.

"Yes, and an elephant — but not a very big one, as you know."

Mr J. L. B. Matekoni asked whether the stockade was ready, and he was assured that it was. "One of the older boys is a very good little carpenter," Mma Potokwani said. "He has built a new gate, and he is fitting that right now. By tonight, everything will be ready."

They spent some time discussing the baby elephant's requirements. Charlie had been feeding it on infant formula, as recommended by his friend, and a large box of this had been obtained from the supermarket. "You must have a very large baby, Rra," said the woman at the checkout when Fanwell had made the purchase. "Looking at you, I wouldn't have thought . . ."

He had said nothing, tempting though it was to reply. The problem was that he had not been able to think of a suitable riposte.

Mma Matlapeng's reply took her by surprise. "We're all sinking, Mma. Even those of us who are floating, are sinking."

Mma Ramotswe was not sure how to respond. To a certain extent, she thought, what Mma Matlapeng said was true: nobody was getting any younger, and that meant that most of us were slowing down, even if imperceptibly. And there was also gravity to be considered: as you went through life, the effects of gravity seemed to get more and more and more pronounced: you felt that, you really did. But even if this were all true, there was no cause to dwell on it, and certainly no reason to say that we were all sinking.

She smiled at her guest. "I don't know about that, Mma," she said. "If we stopped swimming we would certainly sink — but we're not going to stop swimming, are we?"

Mma Matlapeng had been about to say something more, but this remark brought her up short. "That's an interesting way of putting it, Mma," she said. "If we stopped swimming . . ." Her voice trailed off. "Stopped swimming . . ."

Mma Ramotswe felt emboldened. Mma Matlapeng was better educated than she was. She had left school at sixteen, whereas Mma Matlapeng must be a university graduate, with a degree in mathematics, of all subjects. That was impressive by any standards: there were people with degrees that did not involve all that much work, but mathematics . . . So, with the respect that Batswana people feel for education, Mma Ramotswe stood in some awe of a mathematics teacher, but when it came to knowing how to cope with life, then she had no reason to defer to anybody. And now she had said something that had clearly impressed Mma Matlapeng, for all that she had a degree in mathematics. So she said, "Yes, life is like . . ." She paused. The swimming metaphor had come without much thought, but its further development was not proving easy.

"Like swimming?" Mma Matlapeng suggested.

Mma Ramotswe hesitated. That was not what she had been going to say. She had never learned to swim, and she was not sure now why she should say that life was like swimming. It was possible that it was, but on the other hand there were probably many other things that life was like — once you started to think about it.

"Life is like a river," she said at last.

Mma Matlapeng nodded. "I suppose it is. Yes, it is a river, I suppose." She looked at Mma Ramotswe, as if waiting for more, but nothing was said.

Mma Ramotswe looked down at her hands. She stole a glance at Mma Matlapeng. She had learned in life not to make too many snap judgements of people — that, she thought, was one of the main lessons we learned as we got older — but she still found that her initial instincts were often correct. People revealed their characters to you without too much encouragement; you simply had to listen. Or they might do so even without saying very much: in the expression on their face; in the look in their eyes. Eyes, in particular, were revealing. A malevolent disposition always showed in the eyes, in the way in which the light shone out of them. If that light was gentle, if it reassured you, then you could be confident that the person within was of that temper. But if it was hard, if it was hostile, then you could count on there being a character to match within.

For a second or two she watched Mma Matlapeng as her neighbour reached forward to pick up her mug of tea. Their eyes met, very briefly, and the light that she saw in the other woman's was unmistakable.

Mma Ramotswe said, "My husband is away too. Not away away — not in Francistown or anywhere like that — but out in Tlokweng. I am going to have dinner by myself, Mma. I have a chicken in the pot."

Mma Matlapeng smiled. "I smelled it, Mma. I sat here thinking: Mma Ramotswe is going to have chicken for her dinner. She is very lucky." She took a sip of her tea. "Perhaps I should be a detective — like you, Mma."

They laughed.

"Anybody can be a detective," said Mma Ramotswe. "I had no training. But not everybody can be a teacher of mathematics, I think. Certainly not me."

Mma Matlapeng was modest. "It is not all that difficult, Mma. Numbers always behave according to some simple rules. Learn those rules and — *bang!* — you are doing mathematics."

Mma Ramotswe noticed the *bang*. It was the second time Mma Matlapeng had used the word. There had been bankruptcy *bang*, and now there was mathematics *bang*.

Mma Matlapeng referred back to what had been said about training. "Somebody must have taught you something, Mma," she said. "Nobody does a job without at least some training."

"I had a book," said Mma Ramotswe. "There is a very good book on the subject by somebody called Clovis Andersen. He is an American. I know him, actually. He came to Botswana once and my assistant and I met him. Mma Makutsi. She works with me. We both met Mr Andersen."

"And this book tells you everything you need to know?"

Mma Ramotswe nodded. "Yes. He sets out a lot of rules."

"Propositions?"

"Yes, you can call them propositions. They are all about what you should do when investigating a matter for your client. Often they are simply rules of common sense — about how to draw a conclusion, that sort of thing."

"Logic?" suggested Mma Matlapeng.

"Yes. He talks about that, Mma. About not judging people before you have evidence. About not believing what you want to believe rather than paying attention to what your eyes or ears tell you."

Mma Matlapeng said that this all sounded very sensible to her. Then she sniffed at the air and said, "Chicken is one of my favourites. My grandmother used to make us chicken on Sundays. We went to her house and she had a big pot of chicken and she always gave me and my brother the feet."

They both knew what that meant. Chicken feet were the favourite part of the chicken in Botswana.

"You must have been happy," said Mma Ramotswe.

Mma Matlapeng turned to her. "Happy?"

"Yes, you must have been happy at your grandmother's house. With the chicken for lunch, and your grandmother. What else do we need to be happy?"

Mma Matlapeng smiled, and Mma Ramotswe saw that the smile was rueful. She made her decision. "Mma," she said, "I have a whole chicken in the pot, but there is only one of me. My husband will not be back until, oh, ten o'clock — maybe even later. I have made him a beef sandwich. Will you help me eat my chicken?"

"But, Mma, that is very kind of you. I did not mean to ask you . . . When I said that chicken was my favourite dish, I was just thinking. You know how you do, when you smell something, you think about it and may say something? You do not mean to say, 'Can I have some of your food?' I would not say that, Mma."

Mma Ramotswe assured her that she had not thought that — not for a moment. "One chicken is too much for one person," she said. "You should not eat a whole chicken." It was what she had planned to do, but you should always be prepared to change your plans, she told herself. And if the plans had been slightly greedy plans, then you would always feel better after you had changed them.

"Then I will help you, Mma."

"That is very kind of you, Mma."

Mma Matlapeng looked at her watch. "I will go home and get out of these gardening clothes. They are very dusty. Then I will come back."

"We will eat in the kitchen," said Mma Ramotswe. "It is easier that way."

"The best place to eat," said Mma Matlapeng, as she rose to her feet.

They sat at the kitchen table, the pot of chicken between them. The conversation had flowed easily, and Mma Ramotswe had found that her initial impression of Mma Matlapeng was confirmed. She liked her, and found herself wondering whether this was the same woman whom she had heard shouting at her husband. Was this courteous and engaging woman the same person who had been hurling insults, including that colourful comparison with an ant-eater? It was hard to imagine that, and yet, as she had found time and time again in the course of her professional duties, one should never be surprised by anything one found out to be going on in a marriage.

Mma Matlapeng told her more about her background. Her father, she said, had been a school inspector. He was a graduate, in history, of Fort Hare, and could have had a career in politics but had had no stomach for arguments.

"He could never see why people couldn't co-operate," she said. "He said that he could see good points in all the different parties, and yet they were always running one another down."

Mma Ramotswe agreed with that. She thought it ridiculous that party leaders refused to recognise that their opponents could get at least some things right. "And they are so quick to insult one another," she said.

"I can't stand hearing people insult one another, Mma . . ." She stopped herself. She had not intended to stray onto that ground.

Fortunately, Mma Matlapeng did not appear to notice.

"He knew Seretse Khama," she said. "He could have been minister of education in his government, I think, but he wanted to stay in the civil service. He was a civil service man at heart."

"I would not like to be in the government," said Mma Ramotswe. "You would have no peace, I think. Problems, problems, problems — every day. That is what it's like being in the government. You have all these problems and then there are all those people waiting to find fault with what you're doing. You get no thanks."

Mma Matlapeng was of the same view. "If they came to me tomorrow and asked me to be minister of something or other, I would say no. I wouldn't hesitate — I would just say no."

"That would be best," said Mma Ramotswe. Then she asked, "Are you happy in your job, Mma? Do you like teaching mathematics?"

Mma Matlapeng shrugged. "I like most of it. Most people like some bits of their jobs and not others. I like it when I get through to some of the kids. Maybe a child who has not been doing well — who has a confidence problem, maybe — and then you show them that they can actually do mathematics rather well, and then you see their face light up and you know that

249

you've got through to them. That is a very special moment."

"It must be," said Mma Ramotswe.

"I had a boy, fourteen, maybe fifteen; he was not doing very well in my mathematics class, and so I gave him some extra time in the afternoon. And I managed to get out of him what was bothering him — what was holding him back. You know what it was, Mma? It was his own father. His own father was telling him that he was stupid and would never be any good."

Mma Ramotswe shook her head. "There are some very unkind parents," she said. "I don't know why they bother to have children." She paused. "What did you do, Mma?"

"I let him talk to me. Sometimes half the problem with these children is that nobody ever listens to what they want to say. So I sat there and let him tell me. I heard the lot, Mma. All about his father making him feel small. And the father sounded like a thoroughly nasty piece of work — one of these people who step all over other people. You know the sort."

"I do," said Mma Ramotswe, and thought, inevitably, of Violet Sephotho.

"And then a very strange thing happened, Mma," continued Mma Matlapeng. "This arrogant father had a big fall. *Bang!* He went bankrupt. My husband told me that he had been appointed to wind up his affairs. I felt sorry for the family, but I was able to talk to the son about it. I did not want to turn him against his father, but I was able to point out to him that his father had shown that he was human, like everybody else. I think it made all the difference, Mma. He had been in awe of his father for a long time; now he could stand up to him — inside."

"And his mathematics?"

"He started to do very well, Mma. He has gone off now to do a degree in mathematics. He wants to be an actuary. Do you know about actuaries, Mma?"

"They are the people who tell you when you're going to die?"

Mma Matlapeng laughed. "Well, not you personally — but you as a lady of such and such an age, living in such and such a place, and smoking twenty cigarettes a day, or whatever dangerous things you're doing. Not that you smoke, Mma, I'm not accusing you of that, but some people do. Then *bang*, their arteries get clogged up and they become late. The actuaries can say to these people: you are going to last so many more years because that's what the actuarial tables say about somebody like you." She paused. "I'm not sure that it would make me any happier to know when I was going to die, Mma."

Mma Ramotswe agreed with her on that. That was not knowledge that she wanted to have. She said, almost without thinking about it, "Are you happy now, Mma? You said that would not make you any happier . . ."

Mma Matlapeng frowned. "Am I happy now?"

"Yes."

Mma Matlapeng looked away. For some time, she said nothing, and the silence in the kitchen became

noticeable. Then, "You know, Mma, the other day —
did you hear something?"

Mma Ramotswe hesitated, but then made her
decision. "I suppose I did, Mma. I heard . . ."

She was not sure how to put it. A loud discussion? A
little disagreement? There were tactful ways of
describing it, but before she could choose which
expression to use, Mma Matlapeng continued, "I am
very ashamed, Mma. I have only just moved to this
place, and then people hear me shouting." She paused;
she looked shamefaced now. "And everybody will be
thinking: who is this woman who shouts and shouts like
that? That's what they'll be thinking, Mma."

Mma Ramotswe tried to reassure her. "I hardly
heard you, Mma. It was very faint. I really don't think
people will be talking."

Mma Matlapeng reached out and touched Mma
Ramotswe's arm briefly. "You are far too kind, Mma.
I'm afraid I lost control. I shouted."

"We all shout," said Mma Ramotswe. "From time to
time, that is. Is there anybody — anybody, Mma —
who hasn't shouted at one time or another?"

"In private, maybe, Mma. You can shout a little in
private, but you have to keep your voice down. I didn't,
and now I'm very embarrassed, Mma, because you
must be wondering what sort of people have moved in
beside you. I wouldn't be surprised, Mma, if you have
been thinking that we are a very low sort of person."

Mma Ramotswe made a dismissive gesture. "Certainly
not, Mma. I have not been thinking that. Although . . ."
She stopped. She had not intended to say anything

252

about her misgivings, and indeed it would be quite inappropriate to mention the single beds.

"Although what, Mma?"

"Although I did wonder if you and your husband were happy together . . . You seemed very cross with him."

Mma Matlapeng sighed. "I was. I have been very cross with my husband for ten months now."

Mma Ramotswe raised an eyebrow. With her experience of matrimonial investigations, there could be only one reason for that: an errant husband. It was a familiar story.

She looked at Mma Matlapeng, who nodded, as if to confirm the suspicions that she imagined were in Mma Ramotswe's mind. Then she said, "Yes. The usual, Mma."

"Oh."

Mma Matlapeng continued, "I think that one woman does not have to explain these things to another woman. We are all sisters, Mma. We all know how men behave."

Mma Ramotswe was silent for a few moments. Mma Matlapeng was right, of course; all women knew how men behaved. And although she was not one to consign all men to the crowded ranks of philanderers, many men freely and by their own actions enrolled themselves therein. It was something to do with the way men were *inside*. They had to do these things when common sense and caution, not to say loyalty and simple decency, pointed in the other direction. It was not only tragic — it was puzzling.

She lowered her voice. "I take it that your husband has . . . has wandered, Mma. I take it that is what you're saying to me?"

Mma Matlapeng inclined her head. Then she raised it, and gravity of manner was replaced by outrage. "Yes, he has wandered, Mma."

Mma Ramotswe made a clicking sound with her tongue. It was a noise that so many women, all over the world, made when they thought of the behaviour of men. It was a universal gesture. "Men can be very foolish," she said. "I believe it is something to do with their brains."

"I don't think it's their brains," said Mma Matlapeng. "The brain often says stop, but the rest of the man is not listening at that point."

"No, it is in the brain," insisted Mma Ramotswe. "Everything we do, Mma, comes from the brain. The brain says, 'Do this,' and we do it. That is the latest view, Mma."

"Hormones," said Mma Matlapeng. "It is to do with hormones. Hormones are very bad news for men."

"That is true," said Mma Ramotswe. "But the point I'm making, Mma, is that your story must be the commonest story in the country. Up and down the land, there are men being affected by hormones, and doing stupid things." She sighed once more. "We women have to live with it, I'm afraid."

Mma Matlapeng frowned. "Do we? Do we have to put up with this sort of thing? Why, Mma?"

"Because I don't see men changing," said Mma Ramotswe. "We can tell them that we expect better —

254

and that will have some effect — but we are not going to change some things about men. We are not going to be able to change their nature."

"So, we tolerate it?" asked Mma Matlapeng. And then she continued, "So, I have to accept that my husband can go off for a weekend with another woman, Mma? Are you suggesting that?"

"Is that what happened?" asked Mma Ramotswe.

Mma Matlapeng did not answer immediately, and Mma Ramotswe wondered whether her question had been too intrusive. She was about to change the subject when her neighbour suddenly answered, "Yes. It started about a year ago. I found out quite quickly. A wife can always tell."

Mma Ramotswe knew what she meant. Over the years she had listened to any number of women in her office saying exactly that. "You can always tell, Mma," they would say. "A wife is never wrong about that sort of thing. Wives have an instinct for such things." And, by and large, these women who said that were right. Wives could tell, no matter how much their husbands tried to hide what was going on. Women could tell.

"She is another of these bankruptcy people," Mma Matlapeng continued. "She works in a different firm, but she does the same sort of thing as he does. They met when a mine went bankrupt." She gave Mma Ramotswe a sceptical look. "How can a mine go bankrupt, Mma? All you have to do is dig."

"I suppose there are wage bills, Mma," said Mma Ramotswe. "And then perhaps they dig in the wrong place and they have to start again, and that costs money, and so on. Running a business is not easy. At any moment you can discover that you have no money to pay the bills and none of your clients is replying to your reminder that they should pay the invoice you sent them a month ago. And you don't know where to turn . . ."

Mma Matlapeng thought about this. "I suppose you're right, Mma, but anyway, he met this woman and she must have encouraged him. You know how there are some women who *encourage* men, Mma. You know about those women?"

Mma Ramotswe indicated that she did. "There is a well-known woman like that," she said. "There is a certain lady in this town called Violet. She is famous for that sort of thing."

"I have never heard of her," said Mma Matlapeng. "This woman is called Rose."

"They are both names of flowers," mused Mma Ramotswe. "Not that there can be any connection, but it's interesting that they should both have flower names."

Mma Matlapeng tackled a piece of chicken on the side of her plate. "This chicken is very delicious, Mma," she said. "But to get back to this woman. How could she? She knew that he was married. She knew that, and yet she allowed this affair to develop."

"That is what happens, Mma," said Mma Ramotswe. "It is to do with male weakness. Men are weak when it comes to that department, Mma. That is what they are like."

Mma Matlapeng was having none of that. "Well, women should tell them that it is not going to happen. If women said 'I am not going to have anything to do with a married man' then the man would just go home and behave himself." She paused. "I confronted him, Mma. I sat him down in a chair and told him that I knew all about it. He closed his eyes and sank his head in his hands. He said that he would bring it to an end. He said that he did not know what had come over him."

Mma Ramotswe listened. This was not what usually happened. "You were lucky, Mma. Often men just say nothing. Or they deny it all and then the next day they disappear with the other woman. There have been many cases like that."

"I believe that he did as he said he would do," said Mma Matlapeng. "She turned up at the house the following day and tried to claim him. Right in front of my nose, Mma. She didn't seem to mind that I knew. She came and tried to drag him away."

Mma Ramotswe's eyes widened. "That must have been very awkward, Mma."

Mma Matlapeng laughed. "I saw her off," she said. "I was in the kitchen when this happened. He was in the garden — he had been washing his car — when she came and grabbed him. I went outside. We had a hosepipe at the side of the house, and he had been using that. I took it and sprayed her with water. She was completely soaked. She was shouting and swearing, Mma — very bad language — but I just turned up the pressure on the tap and tried to get the water into her mouth. She eventually went away, dripping."

Mma Ramotswe was smiling. She did not approve of violence, but there were times when a bit of gentle force seemed to be justified: people who used bad language should not be surprised if other people came and washed their mouth out with a hosepipe.

"And then I sprayed him too," continued Mma Matlapeng. "Just for good measure. I felt very cross, Mma — I hope you can understand why. I soaked him too, and he just stood there because he was in the wrong and could not do anything about it. If you are in the wrong and somebody sprays you with water, you have to accept it."

Mma Ramotswe was not sure what to say. She could understand how Mma Matlapeng had felt, but she was not certain that this was the way to repair a marriage. So she asked, "And then, Mma?"

"And then?" echoed Mma Matlapeng. "And then I told him what he could expect, Mma. I told him that he could stay in the house if he wanted, but that I would not forget what he had done. And that is where we are now, Mma. He is in disgrace. He is like a dog that has stolen the mince and is in disgrace."

Mma Ramotswe's doubts about the wisdom of this were unassuaged. There was a limit to the extent to which a husband might be punished before it might occur to him to leave. It seemed to her that Mma Matlapeng had embarked on a dangerous strategy. "You have to be careful with husbands," she said.

"They might go away if things are too uncomfortable for them. I have seen that happen, Mma."

"I don't think he will go away," said Mma Matlapeng. "I own the farm, you see."

Mma Ramotswe waited.

"We have a big farm down near Lobatse," Mma Matlapeng explained, a note of triumph in her voice. "We have a house in the town, but we also have a farm. It is probably one of the best farms in that part of the country." She paused, and then, with a smile, continued, "And it's mine, Mma. It belonged to my parents, who are late, and it is now mine."

Mma Ramotswe said nothing, but, having first offered the pot to Mma Matlapeng, she helped herself to a chicken drumstick and a spoonful of sauce. There was more pumpkin and a bowl of rice from which she ladled several spoonfuls onto her plate. Then she topped up their water glasses before she tackled her second helping. She needed to think about what Mma Matlapeng had just said: it was the piece of information that made sense of what she had just heard. It was an old, familiar story of a relationship that had gone wrong but that was limping along because of some outside factor — children or property. And both of these, when one thought about them, amounted to the same thing: dependence.

This situation, she thought, was slightly different from the usual case. It was so often the woman who was obliged to remain in an unhappy marriage or partnership because the man held all the financial cards. Here, it was different — she was well off and even if he, as a bankruptcy accountant, was no doubt comfortably placed, the really important asset was hers. And about time, thought Mma Ramotswe — it was about time that men stopped hoarding all the property and allowed women to have their fair share. It would take years — centuries, perhaps — before there was a just division, but at least things were moving in the right direction.

They ate in silence for a while. Mma Ramotswe noticed that Mma Matlapeng was smiling, as if she were relishing the satisfaction of having an errant husband exactly where she wanted him. Then Mma Ramotswe said, "And what about the future, Mma?"

Mma Matlapeng laid her knife and fork aside. "Very good," she said, and then added, "I mean the chicken is very good, Mma Ramotswe — not the future. Although I don't see anything wrong with the future."

Mma Ramotswe considered this. "The future . . . Well, the future, Mma, is . . . I mean, what about him, Mma?"

"My husband? He'd better watch out, Mma. If he wants a future — *any* future — he'd better watch out."

Mma Ramotswe took a deep breath. There was a question that she wanted to ask, but she was not sure whether this was the time to ask it. Perhaps it was.

"Are you going to forgive him, Mma?"

Mma Matlapeng looked astonished. "Forgive?"

"Yes. Sometimes we do things that we regret. All of us, Mma. We do things and then we think, Oh, goodness, look what I've done. And then we feel very bad about ourselves, and we hope that —"

260

"That nobody notices?"

Mma Ramotswe shook her head. "That was not what I was going to say, Mma. I was going to say, 'And then we hope that people will forgive us.' I think that is what we sometimes hope — often, in fact."

Mma Matlapeng was concentrating on what Mma Ramotswe said. She was listening. And this encouraged Mma Ramotswe to continue, "Forgiveness is very powerful, Mma. It can change things completely. It's like the rain that we long for. Everything is dry, dust everywhere, and then the rain comes. You smell it coming and suddenly it is there and it changes everything. You know what that is like, Mma — the first rains."

Mma Matlapeng was clearly struggling. "I don't see what the rain has to do with it, Mma," she said. "People still behave badly when it rains."

Mma Ramotswe shook her head. "That's not the point, Mma. I'm saying that forgiveness is *like* the rain. That's all I'm saying. It makes things better. Rain does that too. Things grow . . ."

Mma Matlapeng went off on another tack. "But if you forgive people, Mma Ramotswe, then you know what happens?" She did not let Mma Ramotswe respond, but went on to answer her own question. "If you forgive them, they say, 'Good, now I can go and do it again.' I'm telling you, Mma — that's how people think. It's just like that in the classroom: you have an unruly pupil and you let him off. The next moment, when you turn your back, he does the same thing again. That's the way it is, Mma."

Mma Ramotswe looked at her plate, now wiped clean. They had finished the chicken, the two of them, and it was time for a fat cake, dusted in sugar, and a cup of tea perhaps. She offered these to Mma Matlapeng, who accepted with enthusiasm. "This has been a wonderful dinner, Mma Ramotswe. You are a very good cook, I think."

Mma Ramotswe took the fat cakes out of the fridge and set them out on two plates. She took a bite, watched by Mma Matlapeng, who was removing excess sugar off the first of her cakes.

"No," said Mma Matlapeng, as she licked the tip of a finger. "If you go round forgiving people, then they will be very pleased and will do it again."

She looked at Mma Ramotswe challengingly as she said this, and Mma Ramotswe almost gave up. But then she thought of Bishop Mwamba, and of what he had said about forgiveness. His words had never left her; she had heard them in the cathedral opposite the hospital, on a warm Sunday morning, with the great ceiling fans above their heads turning slowly. He had said, "It is our duty to forgive because if we do not, then we sentence ourselves to the repetition of the very things we want to avoid." And she had thought at the time, yes, that is right: if you forgive somebody, then normal life can resume. You start again.

So she said to Mma Matlapeng, "We have to forgive, Mma, because it is wrong to hold something against somebody forever."

Mma Matlapeng was studying her fat cake, poised before her lips. She hesitated.

262

"We have to, Mma," Mma Ramotswe continued. "Because it's cruel to make somebody suffer more than they deserve. Forgiveness stops that."

Mma Matlapeng continued to study the fat cake. She opened her mouth and took a bite.

"Is that what you really think, Mma?" she said.

"Yes," said Mma Ramotswe.

She picked up a fat cake and popped it into her mouth. She could no longer talk now, nor could Mma Matlapeng, and so they finished the fat cakes, their mouths full of pleasure.

"Look at the time," said Mma Matlapeng at last. "I must go home, Mma. I've enjoyed myself very much, thank you."

Mma Ramotswe saw her guest out as far as the gate. Then she turned and walked back to the house, through the cool of the evening. Above her, high above her, the constellations of the African sky dipped and swung against the darkness of the night.

CHAPTER
FOURTEEN

This Is a Big Mess

Mma Makutsi could not contain herself. She arrived early at the office the following morning — a good half an hour before Mma Ramotswe — and had tidied the desks, opened the windows and switched on the kettle by the time Mma Ramotswe's white van swung off the road and was securely parked in its place under the acacia tree.

"You are very early today," Mma Ramotswe remarked as she entered the office and hung her scarf on the back of her chair. "A lot of the birds are still in their beds in the trees, and yet the office is already up and running!" She heard the asthmatic hissing of the kettle, and she smiled. "And I see that the kettle is already heating up. That is all very good, Mma."

Mma Makutsi waved a hand airily. "Phuti made an early start today too," she said. "He's expecting a big consignment of furniture from over the border and he likes to be there when they unpack it. He says some of the men are very careless."

Mma Ramotswe shook her head. "It's a shame, isn't it, Mma Makutsi, that people treat other people's property like that. I think that if something doesn't belong to you, you should be —"

She did not finish. Mma Makutsi waved her hand again. "Yes, yes, Mma. You're right about that. We should all be careful." She paused, and then added, "All the time. We should be careful all the time. But tell me, Mma: what happened? I'm very keen to hear."

"I shall tell you, Mma," said Mma Ramotswe. She looked at the kettle. "That kettle is very old. It takes more and more time to boil. I think that soon we'll have to switch it on when we leave the office the day before so that the water is boiling by the time we arrive in the morning."

Mma Makutsi sucked in her cheeks. "Maybe. Maybe. But I was wondering, Mma . . ."

Mma Ramotswe was not deliberately dragging her feet, but she had noticed something different about Mma Makutsi and now realised what it was. "Your new glasses, Mma," she exclaimed. "You've abandoned your new glasses."

Mma Makutsi's hand shot up to adjust her old, familiar glasses. "I've decided that this pair is still useful, Mma," she said. "I'll keep the other pair for special occasions — when it's important to be fashionable. These will do for everything else."

Mma Ramotswe suppressed a smile. It was always satisfying to her when functionality won over fashion. In her mind, all the fuss over designer labels was a distraction from the main issue, which was comfort. Things should be comfortable. Shoes should not pinch your feet; glasses should not sit awkwardly on the nose;

265

blouses should not bunch up at the armpits; dresses should not cling to your skin but allow air to circulate freely on a hot day. Mma Makutsi had good dress sense — even if she tended to prefer colours that were rather too bright, and occasionally clashing — but she was far too easily swayed by the cajolery of commerce. If something was said to be "the latest thing" then you could be sure that Mma Makutsi would take such a claim seriously, whereas Mma Ramotswe would simply laugh and point out that latest things did not seem to last very long and that many of them, anyway, were instantly recognisable as "the latest thing" of some years previously, and were now being recycled to a gullible public.

"I like those glasses," she said. "I mean, these old . . . or, rather, these traditional glasses of yours. I like them a bit more than those new, fashionable ones."

Mma Makutsi got up from her desk to attend to the kettle, which was now emitting cloudlets of steam from its spout. "This is a very stupid kettle," she said. "But, Mma, let's not talk about kettles and glasses and things. What I am very keen to hear is what happened last night out at Mma Potokwani's place. That is what I want to hear." She paused. "And where is Mr J. L. B. Matekoni? And Charlie and Fanwell? Where are all the men?"

Mma Ramotswe laughed. "That would be a good title for a song, Mma, don't you think? 'Where Are All the Men?' It would be a song that many ladies would sing, I think. *Where are all the men, la, la, la? Where are all the men?*"

266

Mma Makutsi had no time for such frippery. "Mma, you must tell me. I'm bursting now. I'm bursting with curiosity. Did they move that little elephant?"

Mma Ramotswe sat back in her chair. "They did, Mma. It all went very well — or rather, it went very well after it went badly. At first it went very badly and then . . . well, then, things got better and it went well. Now, I think, it is all going very well again."

Mma Makutsi poured the hot water into the two teapots — one containing redbush tea for Mma Ramotswe, and the other containing Five Roses tea for herself.

"Mr J. L. B. Matekoni will be in shortly," said Mma Ramotswe. "But I think that Charlie and Fanwell are not expected in until ten o'clock. They were all very late last night, and Mr J. L. B. Matekoni told them they did not need to come in until later. They will be having a long sleep. It was two o'clock, you see, by the time Mr J. L. B. Matekoni got home."

Mma Makutsi registered her surprise. "Two o'clock, Mma! What happened? You must tell me."

She poured them each a mug of tea and then settled in the client's chair, facing Mma Ramotswe across her desk.

Mma Ramotswe took her first sip of redbush tea. "He was very tired when he got home. I was asleep, but I always wake up if somebody comes into the room. He said that I should go back to sleep as everything was all right and I did not need to worry. But I was awake by then, and so I got him to tell me exactly what had happened."

"Which was what, Mma?"

"Which was that they had an accident on the way to Mma Potokwani's. My poor van, Mma, it has more scrapes down the side from toppling into a ditch. The elephant moved, you see, and that disturbed the van's balance."

"Oh, Mma!" exclaimed Mma Makutsi. "I'm so sorry to hear that. Your poor van is being trampled by elephants and then driven into a ditch. And then there are its suspension troubles . . . How much more can it bear?"

"It is very strong," said Mma Ramotswe. "That van has a very strong heart inside it. It will be all right."

"So what happened then, Mma?"

Mma Ramotswe explained how the accident had occurred very near the Orphan Farm and how they had managed to complete the trip after righting the van. "Without the baby elephant, of course. It had run off into the bush and it was very dark. They could not see where it had gone and so they went to tell Mma Potokwani about what had happened."

"And she said?"

"She said that Charlie should go out into the bush to wait for the elephant to come to him. She said that these little elephants think that the person looking after them is their mother. She said that this would bring him back to Charlie."

Mma Makutsi listened in fascination. "They are very strange creatures," she said. "They think just like us. They have very large brains, I believe."

Mma Ramotswe continued her account. "Mr J. L. B. Matekoni eventually went out with the two boys. Young men, of course — they are no longer boys."

"Sometimes," said Mma Makutsi.

"Anyway, he did not want them to get lost or get into some sort of trouble, and so he went with them in the end. And they wandered about through the bush — rather them than me, Mma."

"Me too," agreed Mma Makutsi, with a shiver.

"And then, after hours and hours, the little elephant suddenly appeared from behind some trees and rushed up to Charlie. They had its bottle with them and they gave it the formula they've been feeding it. It was very thirsty, and they used the bottle to make sure it stayed with them on the way back to the Orphan Farm. Then they put it in the cattle stockade that Mma Potokwani had fixed up for them, and that's where it is right now."

Mma Makutsi, who had been on the edge of her seat during this story, sat back. "Well, well," she said. "That is a very good ending, Mma." She hesitated. "But what now?"

"Mma Potokwani has been in touch with her friend up north. There is an American lady who has a place up near Maun. They look after elephants that have lost their mothers. She is sending a truck. They'll take it up there. They'll give it a home."

Mma Makutsi picked up her mug. "I'm pleased, Mma."

"So am I," said Mma Ramotswe.

She looked out of the window, at the patch of sky it revealed. Had it darkened? She thought perhaps it had, and she stood up to get a better view.

"Take a look up there," she said to Mma Makutsi. "Do you think those are rain clouds, Mma — or do you think it's just the heat?"

Mma Makutsi stood up. She adjusted her glasses, her large, round glasses, and for a moment Mma Ramotswe saw herself reflected in the lenses. So that, she thought, is what Mma Makutsi sees when she looks at me.

"I think that might be rain," said Mma Makutsi. "Yes, I think so. I hope so."

They finished their tea.

"We have some difficult business today," said Mma Ramotswe, as she drained her cup. "I've been trying not to think about it, but I'll have to do something, I'm afraid. And I was hoping that you would come and help me, Mma."

Mma Makutsi knew immediately what it was. "Blessing?" she asked.

"Yes," said Mma Ramotswe. "I'm going to have to go and see her."

Mma Makutsi waited, but then she prompted, "And sort it out, Mma?"

Mma Ramotswe bit her lip. "I have to. I can't ignore her. She's a cousin — even if a very remote one."

Mma Makutsi sighed. "They're trying to trick you, Mma. That man is acting."

"But you heard from the magistrate. She told you. He really was convicted."

"Yes, but . . . But even if that part of the story is true, this business about the operation is obviously a lie. It's a trick to get you to make you give them money. That's all it is, Mma." She looked at Mma Ramotswe. This good woman, this generous woman, was obviously a tempting target for a couple of confidence tricksters. But such people always were: good people were the ideal victims.

Mma Ramotswe was decisive. "We need to go down there," she said.

Mma Makutsi glanced out of the window. "What if it rains? That road down there will be difficult."

Mma Ramotswe was confident. "My van has had worse things happen to it," she said, with a grin. "And so have we, Mma Makutsi."

Mma Makutsi was largely silent on the way down to Blessing's village. Mma Ramotswe knew the reason for this: when her colleague had misgivings about something, she usually expressed these through silence. This, in a way, was a far more eloquent way of expressing opposition than by saying directly why she felt as she did. And now, as the tiny white van bumped its way along the rough track to the village, the silence was a pointed one.

The sky had darkened behind them as they set off on the Lobatse Road; large purple clouds, heavy with rain, had stacked up in the north-west and were moving slowly south. The intentions of these clouds were clear enough: within a short time, a few hours at the most, they would discharge their liquid burden in a heavy deluge. The sky would become white with rain, falling in great curtain sweeps across the land, blown into lashing, cleansing showers. And when that happened, the very earth would seem to leap up into the embrace of the longed-for rain, with dust and soil being confused in a brown blur. Tracks like the one they were on would become seas of mud, with puddles like minor lakes stretching across fields, bordered by ditches that had become narrow fast-flowing rivers. But that had not yet happened as Mma Ramotswe drew up in front of Blessing's house and suggested to Mma Makutsi that they should watch the time. "Twenty minutes at the most, Mma," she said, glancing over her shoulder at the storm clouds.

"If that," muttered Mma Makutsi.

They had been spotted, and as they made their way up the front path, Blessing appeared in the doorway.

She appeared to be surprised. "Mma Ramotswe!" she exclaimed. "And Mma Makutsi too. You are bringing us rain. *Pula! Pula! Pula!*" The Setswana word for rain was also the word for good luck — and repeated thus was an invocation of good fortune. It also meant "money", of course, but in these circumstances, Mma Ramotswe thought, that was a bit unfortunate.

They went inside, where Blessing offered them tea. From the room off the living room, a cough was heard.

"That is my mother," said Blessing. "She is sleeping today, but she still coughs in her sleep. She does not wake up so much these days."

"I thought that I should come to see you, Mma," said Mma Ramotswe. "I needed to talk to you in person."

"You are always welcome, Mma," said Blessing, her gaze shifting anxiously from Mma Ramotswe to Mma Makutsi, and then back again.

Mma Ramotswe clasped her hands together. She knew what she had to do, but she was not finding it easy.

"You came to see me about Tefo," she said.

"Yes," said Blessing. "The cousin."

Mma Makutsi exchanged glances with Mma Ramotswe.

"Yes," said Mma Ramotswe. "But he is also your friend, isn't he? Your husband, maybe."

Blessing lowered her gaze. "He is not a close cousin, Mma."

"That is not my business," said Mma Ramotswe.

"You can marry somebody who is not a very close cousin," said Blessing, her voice rising.

"I know that, Mma," said Mma Ramotswe calmly. "But I didn't come to talk about that. I came to tell you why I can't help. I think I must tell you that, rather than ignore your cry for help. You are my cousin and I must speak to you directly."

Blessing was tight-lipped.

"We do not think that Tefo really needs an operation, Mma. We think that you are trying to get money from me for some other reason."

She sat back. She had said it.